The Honu Diary

Cover design by Elizabeth Mackey

Developmental Editor Brianne Vander Neut

Dedication

To Chris my soulmate and partner-in-crime

To Hawaii and its amazing natives on both land and in water…
aloha wau ia oe

Contents

Chapter One

"Hey, babe, your sugar mama is on the phone!"

I opened my eyes to see Rodrigo standing over me, smiling and waving my cell phone at me. *What time was it?* He handed me my cell phone, and I heard my bestie Kailani's cheerful voice.

"Hey, sleepyhead. I'm canceling our staff meeting this morning. I'm stuck in Hilo at Sack and Save."

"I meant to send over the financial reports earlier… *sorry.*"

"It's all good. Are you okay? You still sound congested."

"I'm *better*," I wheezed out, then cleared my throat noisily. "I can't believe I'm still sick with this stupid cold."

"You're probably purging old energy. Your body needs some more rest, that's all."

I let out a loud sneeze and quickly ran the back of my hand over my nose.

"Go to the kitchen and get some fresh OJ. And… Shara's baking her famous mango muffins. You better get some before the guests scarf them all down."

"Thanks for the heads up."

"Drink some peppermint tea, too."

I sat up in bed and surveyed the bedroom. A large, dark wood ceiling fan churned slowly above the bed, pushing warm, humid air around the room. The queen-sized cherry wood futon bed barely fit into the small space. A wicker table lamp designed as a palm tree sat on a matching cherry, two-drawer night stand next to the bed. There was a tall, oscillating floor fan at the foot of the bed, which provided some relief at night.

I struggled to get up and padded groggily into the kitchen. I stood over the kitchen sink, which also served as a bathroom sink, and splashed cold water on my face, running my fingers through my tousled, short hair. I'd lopped off most of my shoulder-length hair to a layered pixie bob. It was easier to maintain in a hot and muggy climate. One year earlier, I had been casually dating Rodrigo and living in the San Francisco Bay Area. Now we were engaged and living in Hawaii at a remote yoga retreat in the jungle. I wondered how we'd tolerated the busyness of urban life back in the Bay Area. Yet I missed the billowy, cool fog, Trader Joe's and indoor plumbing.

Rodrigo was busy brewing coffee at the kitchen counter, using his ever-present French press. The tantalizing smell of freshly brewed coffee wafted throughout the modest cottage. He looked up and grinned at me, and my heart fluttered. That irresistible, boyish smile lit up his face. If I wasn't so sick, I would have dragged him back into bed.

"Hey, Sweetie," he said.

"Hey yourself!"

He leaned over and kissed my forehead.

It was still a surprise to wake up to this handsome, sexy, younger man. Yet I occasionally dreamt about my ex-husband, Jason. You'd think after being with Rodrigo for over a year, Jason would be a distant memory, but we'd been together for over twenty years.

Rodrigo busied himself at the sink, washing the previous night's dishes, and I shuffled to the back door, toward the outhouse.

The compost toilet was outside our back door in a bona fide outhouse with an adjoining outdoor shower. It wasn't the most convenient place to stumble to in the middle of the night with a full bladder.

Rodrigo cheerfully whistled the Beatles song "Here Comes the Sun" as I pushed open the screen door, the hinges squeaking and the door slamming shut abruptly behind me with a bang. There was a bucket of cedar sawdust and a stack of magazines inside the outhouse door, along with a neat stack of brown toilet paper. I sat down and relieved myself as a strong breeze jostled the metal, tubular windchimes outside. The pleasant ring was soothing to hear.

I looked down to see a bright, lime-green Gecko lizard scamper in front of my bare feet. I shuddered as I grimly recalled the three-inch flying cockroach that had dive-bombed my face recently.

When I was done, I took a handful of cedar sawdust and threw it into the toilet, then went back into the small, immaculate kitchen. The pungent smell of tea tree oil cleanser wafted up from the shiny, blue, marble kitchen counter. I marveled at how compact and efficient the tiny kitchen was. To the left of the two-burner stove, a narrow, wood bookcase served as storage for plates, glasses, and on the top shelf, glass mason jars held metal utensils. On the other side of the stove, a white, metal peg board supported coffee mugs hung on hooks.

Rodrigo placed two mugs on the kitchen table, then pulled me in for an affectionate hug and kissed the top of my head.

"My poor, sick baby."

There were so many discoveries I'd made about living with Rodrigo that surprised me. Number one was his coffee obsession. I spied his expensive Yeti brand French press on the kitchen counter. There was a bag of local Kona coffee beans next to it, as well as a coffee bean grinder. Before we moved here, I had sold or donated most of my things. One of the casualties was my prized Technivorm coffeemaker, a wedding gift from my former marriage. I felt disproportionately sad about donating it to Goodwill. Mainly because it was the last connection to Jason. Oddly, I'd sold my wedding and engagement ring without remorse. The coffeemaker was just a sentimental reminder of my old,, settled life. My divorce wasn't a *one and done* event but a slow releasing of memories and moments.

"Did you see the wedding photographer links I sent you? We should start interviewing." Rodrigo said.

His voice snapped me out of my nostalgic reverie.

"Not yet. We've got months still."

"*Three* months, to be exact."

"I'll look today."

"You didn't say anything about that honeymoon package I sent you from the Ritz Carlton."

"I thought we were staying at Shara's condo on Maui? She's gifting that to us as our wedding present. It's *free*."

"This is our honeymoon. I heard they have an awesome Lomi Lomi couples massage!" Rodrigo beamed with happiness. He was like a child on Christmas morning.

"I did see that email about the Ritz Carlton. That package deal was like six thousand dollars for a week!"

"I put aside ten grand for our wedding and honeymoon. We're saving money since we're getting married here at the lodge."

Ten thousand? Where did that money come from?

Before I could ask the question, Rodrigo said, "I'm thinking of selling my Dad's Corvette. It's been sitting in storage for two years."

"But… you always dreamed of restoring it."

He shrugged. "Dad got it dirt cheap from a neighbor, but it turns out it needs a lot of work." He reached across the table and squeezed my hand. "Besides… dreams change. I know Dad would approve. Even though he wasn't around a lot, he always told me to follow my heart. He would have loved you!"

I didn't respond. I also didn't want to admit I'd put off looking at wedding stuff because I'd been preoccupied with an unexpected email from Jason. He'd written to inform me he was coming to Hawaii to scatter his mother's ashes. His feisty, ninety year old mother, Virginia, had died a month ago. He'd sent me a copy of her obituary. Ginnie was her preferred name, and after the divorce, she wrote me a Hallmark card written in her distinctive, brassy voice.

*"I love you like a daughter. Please stay in touch. My son is a selfish s**t like my former husband. I know you tried your best to make it work but it was a lost cause. Trust me… I know!"*

I knew Rodrigo wouldn't care if I went to pay my final respects. He'd be more upset that my former husband would be in such close proximity to me. It'd been a year since I last saw Jason, and it hadn't been pleasant.

I wondered which was worse… confiding to your lover you were a changeling or telling him you wanted to go to your former mother-in-law's memorial service? I decided to tell Rodrigo about the memorial first. Rodrigo sat down across from me with his coffee mug and looked at me with his eyebrows raised.

"*What*?" I asked.

"Nothing. Just happy being here with you and our new life together. Sometimes you seem… I don't know, *distracted*. If something's bothering you, I'm here for you."

He reached out and put his hand over mine, gazing at me with his big, puppy brown eyes. I heard my phone's notification beep and repressed the urge to pick it up.

"I'm trying to be a good partner," he added.

"You are a good partner."

I withdrew my hand and tucked a lock of stray hair behind my ear. This was another odd thing. I guess having been married before, you developed a kind of telepathy and cadence. In the first six months after we'd moved here, it felt like Rodrigo was always quizzing me on my state of being. I wasn't used to having a partner who actually checked in with me. Or a partner who worshipped my body. Rodrigo liked to give me massages with warm coconut oil. I was self-conscious when he gently kneaded my round stomach or my jiggly derriere. *How did I get so old?* I remembered when I used to prance around in a bikini, showing off my toned, twenty-something body. *At least my breasts are still perky.*

"You're a thousand miles away," Rodrigo prompted.

"Sorry. I didn't sleep great."

"Night sweats again?"

I nodded. That was partially true. How could I share that I still dreamt about my ex-husband? They were mostly nightmares, *but still.* Yet I also had run out of my BHRT cream that I put on nightly. Besides hormone cream, Rodrigo was amused with my nighttime rituals of peptide night masks, hyaluronic face cream, caffeine eye cream, and magnesium spray on my feet

"I thought Shara's herbal tinctures were helping with the insomnia?"

"They help, but I ran out of my hormone cream. I ordered some more."

"Can't you get some in town?"

"I get them at a compounding pharmacy in San Francisco. It'll be here any day."

Rodrigo looked perplexed. "I'm glad I'm not a woman."

"I'm going over to the lodge to get another bottle of tincture. Shara's also making her famous mango muffins. I better run over there before they disappear. We have a full lodge, and I'm sure the natives will be restless and hungry soon!"

"I'll come with you."

"Relax and enjoy your coffee. I'll be quick!"

"You just want some girl time with Shara. I get it."

I raised my eyebrows. "That's not necessarily true," I protested.

"You don't think I've noticed how the last few times you tried to book some girlfriend time with Kailani, she's put you off? Not intentionally. But you get this tone like… *That's okay. We'll do it some other time.*"

I didn't like the falsetto voice he used to mimic me, and I frowned.

"You've been eavesdropping?"

"Look at our place."

He gestured at our modest cottage. I sighed in resignation.

"Yes. It's true."

"Kailani is like family, I get it."

"She *is* my family. I regret neglecting our friendship when I was with Jason. I was hoping to make up for lost time after we moved here."

"You think about sitting with her and telling her how you feel?"

I shrugged. "She's been really busy."

"It helps to clear the air sometimes is all I'm saying. Transparency builds trust."

I bit my lip at his latter words. *Transparency.*

"Thanks for understanding."

Rodrigo winked at me. "Always."

I got up and went to the door, slipping out, the screen door slamming shut hard behind me as I put on my sandals.

The lodge kitchen was only about ten minutes away. My sandals crunched noisily along the narrow, gravel path. The pleasant sound of chirping birds filled the air, as well as the occasional cawing of the lodge peacock. My loose, cotton t-shirt and baggy cotton shorts were cooling against the humidity. I swiped my damp forehead with the back of my already sticky hand.

Rodrigo was right. With the recent popularity of the lodge, Kailani and Shara were constantly busy. The few moments I had with Kailani was reduced to helping in the kitchen. The fantasy I had about moving here and spending more time with my bestie hadn't panned out. I hid my disappointment by keeping busy and pretending everything was fine. Instead, I should have openly shared my feelings. Hadn't I spent countless sessions with my therapist Dr. Serena discussing the importance of taking risks by being honest about my feelings? It seemed that was something I still needed to work on.

As I got closer to the kitchen, the enticing smell of sugary, freshly baked goods wafted toward me. The thought of warm muffins with butter made me quicken my steps.

When I opened the kitchen door, Shara was taking out two metal muffin tins from the oven.

"Morning!" I said.

She looked up with a warm smile, wearing a white cotton tank top with the lodge logo, over loose, gray yoga pants. It was hard to believe she was a fifty-year-old mother of three. She was toned with muscled shoulders and flat abs. Her honey-blonde hair was styled in a loose topknot, and her face was smooth and tanned. Except for some minor crows feet at the corners of her hazel eyes, she could have easily passed for thirty. She took off the oven mitts and hurried over to me, giving me a quick hug and kiss. Her touchy-feely nature took some getting used to in the beginning, but now I looked forward to it.

"Hey, Sweetie. Ready for some muffins?"

I pulled out a wooden high stool from the countertop and sat down, spying two sticks of yellow butter sitting on a glass plate.

"You sure it's vegan friendly?"

She laughed. "The kids are tired of me being so picky, so I've had to be more flexible. Plus, my youngest loves butter, and my ex-husband—well, I'm not going *there*. You gotta pick your battles." She pulled up a stool next to me. "How are you love birds? Rodrigo is such a dear. He hauled all the trash to the transfer station the other day. I didn't even ask him, he just did it. Having you two here has been a blessing."

"Rodrigo loves it here. The no meat policy threw him off at first, but he's adapting."

Shara waved a dismissive hand. "Don't worry about that. I told him it only applies to the lodge kitchen. What you guys eat in your cabin is your business. You don't think I know Kailani goes on hamburger runs in Hilo?"

I sneezed, and Shara jumped up to grab some paper napkins.

"That cold is really hanging on," she said as she handed me the tissues.

"I'm actually feeling better. The worst part is when I sneeze, I have leakage."

"Oh, that's such a pain. My mother has that."

"I'm leaking *and* turning into a catfish!" I pointed at the wispy hairs on my chin, which I dutifully plucked weekly, hoping Rodrigo wouldn't notice.

Shara chuckled. "The joys of menopause. At least your lady parts aren't all dried up."

"No, but my hair nearly all fell out after the divorce." I self-consciously patted the back of my head. "I used to have thick, full hair, and now I have wispy hair like on those Danish troll dolls. It gets frizzy so easily." I sighed.

"Oh you… that's so funny. The kids used to have those dolls. Hey, how're the wedding plans coming along?"

"Rodrigo's planning all of it. I wanted to elope, but he's never had a wedding. He's really getting into it. I had to insist we cut off the guest list at fifty. I never realized I was marrying into such a large, extended family."

"I get it. I'm an only child, and Kailani's got aunties, uncles, and cousins coming out of the woodwork."

"I know it's a few months away, but I just got divorced. It feels like it's happening too quickly," I stammered.

Shara turned and looked at me. "What's going on? Are you having second thoughts?"

I shook my head. "No. It's just that… we're together twenty-four seven. It just feels weird that he's always underfoot. I wonder if we rushed into this too soon. First, we were dating, and he'd go to work in the morning and I had my alone time."

"You had your own routine. I get that. I think you're just not used to being with someone who obviously adores you!"

Shara's comment jarred something loose in my brain. It was Aunt Lily who's always told me not to trust lasting happiness. I'd carried that belief throughout my life. How long-term happiness seemed to be a fleeting event, not something I could count on. I blurted this out to Shara, and she raised her eyebrows.

"I never met your Aunt Lilly, but from what Kailani told me, she wasn't a happy person. What would Dr. Serena say?"

"She'd tell me to live in the moment."

"There you go!" Shara replied brightly. She went back to the oven and took out trays of mango muffins. The front door opened again, and two hungry guests poked their heads in. Shara waved them in, smiling. "Mango muffins and coffee!" she sang out.

She was in her element as she happily busied herself with serving the guests. I admired how animated she was as she made cheerful small talk. I wasn't feeling sociable, so I grabbed two muffins and slipped out.

Chapter Two

As the kitchen door slammed shut behind me, I looked up to see Lono's pickup truck trundling down the gravel driveway. A spark of joy bloomed in my chest as he pulled up alongside me. He climbed out, wearing his usual black San Francisco Giants tank top over khaki cargo shorts and black flip flops. His thick black hair was tucked under a matching black ball cap. He hurried over to me and swept me up in a tight bear hug.

"Aunty!"

Aunty? I inwardly winced at the respectful title commonly bestowed on older women. What happened to *Sista!*

"Where's your man?"

I waved at hand toward our cabin. "Enjoying his coffee. What're you doing here?"

"Helping Nakoa with his egg deliveries. His truck is in the shop."

"Nakoa… the egg man?"

"The one and only!" Lono joked. I heard the truck door slam shut, and Nakoa emerged from the passenger side of Lono's truck. He was tall and lean with a long, tanned face and shoulder-length salt and pepper hair neatly pulled back in a ponytail. He sported a white Egg Man logo t-shirt over beige cargo shorts. It was a cartoon depiction of a chicken on a surfboard. I guessed he was in his early sixties.

"We haven't officially met… I'm Noelani," I said.

"Nakoa." He extended his hand in greeting, and I shook it as he clasped his other hand over mine warmly. Then something strange happened. The truck and Lono faded away, and Nakoa was years younger, with glossy black hair. I felt an electric jolt shoot through my hand.

Nakoa grinned and said softly, *"You have the gift."*

"You okay, Aunty?" Lono asked.

His voice snapped me back into reality.

"I'm fine."

"I remember you from Dr. Serena's holiday party," Nakoa said. "She and I used to teach yoga together back in Cali."

"What a small world!" I said.

Nakoa turned toward me. "I hear Dr. Serena will be here to officiate at your wedding."

"That's right. You should come to the wedding. Dr. Serena would love to see you, I'm sure!"

Nakoa smiled. "That's very kind of you. I'd love to attend your special day."

Lono shuffled past us with an armload of boxed eggs. "We gotta keep going, Unko, we've got more deliveries."

Shara poked her head out from the kitchen doorway and waved at Nakoa with a smile. "Hi, Unko!" Then she waved me over. "Can you do me a big favor? I can't believe this… but we're almost out of toilet paper in the bath house. Kailani's not answering her phone… could you or Rodrigo run over there or to Sack and Save?"

I nodded. "Sure, no problem."

Shara leaned in for a quick hug. "You guys are lifesavers!"

As Lono pushed past me with an armload of eggs, the word aunty jabbed at me. I wasn't ready to be an aunty!

***

Rodrigo and I drove into Hilo together after noshing on at least three mango muffins. He dropped me off at Carlsmith Beach while he went to Costco to get the toilet paper. I walked along the rock wall of the beach, enjoying the rippling, gray-blue water and briny smell of the ocean.

I wandered to Lono's cove and peered down over the rocky edge, expecting to see him in his *Honu* turtle form. I didn't see anything except foamy water and sat down on the rough ground cross-legged. I had felt his energetic summons. If he was nearby, I felt a brief, itchy feeling on my scalp, but if he was further away, it was a pleasant rippling sensation that fanned over my skin. Maybe it was the Honu version of butt dialing?

"Hey, *girl!*"

I looked up to see Kailani walking toward me with a big smile. She was wearing her usual outfit—short denim overalls over a cotton t-shirt and flip flops. She had on wraparound Oakley sunglasses, which she took off when she plopped down next to me. She leaned over and patted my back fondly.

"What're you doing here?" I asked.

"I saw Rodrigo looking for parking at Costco. He told me he just dropped you off. How's my favorite *mano*?"

It felt funny to called a shark in Hawaiian. I was still adjusting to that identity. "I felt Lono summoning me, but I don't know where he is?"

"He's probably running on turtle time!" Kailani joked. "By the way, I have great news…we just hired a yoga instructor, who is also an amazing massage therapist. His name's Braydon. That frees up my schedule since I'm handing over the yoga classes to him. I know we haven't been able to hang out very much." She reached over to pat my back. "I miss hanging out with you."

I shrugged and looked away. "Business is booming… I get that."

"Don't you miss *me*?"

My cheeks reddened. "*Of course* I do. So, where'd you find Braydon?"

"He's a friend of Lono's. They met at a kambo ceremony."

"Of course they did."

"You have something against licking frogs?" Kailani joked.

"They *lick* the frogs?"

Kailani laughed at my wide-eyed expression. "No, of course not. A practitioner applies the poison to the skin."

"*Okay*. So, you hired someone Lono met at a frog licking ceremony?"

Kailani rolled her eyes. "No… I actually interviewed him over Zoom and checked his references. He's got good energy—you'll like him."

"Are you going to be offering organic Kambo smoothies at the lodge?"

She poked me playfully. "What's up with you? Are you and Rodrigo okay?"

"We're fine."

"You seem distracted these days."

"What do you mean?"

"Shara mentioned you didn't seem that excited about planning the wedding."

I sighed. "I'm feeling overwhelmed. I haven't told Rodrigo about my *mano* self or even that Jason is coming to scatter his mother's ashes. I feel bad about keeping all that from him."

"So, just tell him."

"I'm more worried about Jason coming than about my mano confession."

"*Seriously?* Do you want me to talk to Rodrigo for you?"

"That would make it ten times worse!"

"I don't think Rodrigo would care if you go to your former mother-in-law's memorial service. Or is it something else?"

I shrugged. "Dr. Serena has told me I struggle with trusting happiness. Aunt Lily's mantra was… *I'm just waiting for the other shoe to drop.* All my life, she warned me about jinxing myself by expecting lasting happiness."

"Dr. Serena also said you never embraced being a Highly Sensitive Person and an Empath. How you always had to be perfect to get your aunty's approval. It's the original mother wound."

Mother wound. Dr. Serena had said that to me years ago. I could still remember the softness in her voice and her kind eyes. *"You had to earn love. You had to be good, to not have needs, to keep safe by being a model child. It's tough to always be in survival mode."* My face had gone hot at her words. A jab of shame lanced me in the gut. Now Kailani's well-meaning words triggered that humiliation again.

"I was the same way, so I get it. My mother wanted me to be a *muggle* like her. She was afraid for me because of my paranormal powers. I never told you this… but I saw your aunt at her memorial service. She spoke to me." Goosebumps fanned down both my arms. "She waved at me and said how proud she was of you. She said she could leave and be at peace finally."

I shook my head in disbelief. "Why didn't you tell me this before?"

"She told me to wait until the perfect time. You were pretty distraught, and I didn't feel you were ready."

I folded my arms over my chest and took in a long, deep breath, looking down at the wet, rocky ground. It was hard to imagine Aunt Lily saying something so kind. The last vivid memory I had of her was donating her gold, wire, half-moon reading glasses to Goodwill. As I put them in the donation box along with her clothes, it triggered unhappy memories of her peering over the rims, her brows knitted with displeasure.

"She never said anything like that to me."

"She wanted you to let go of the past. I'm sure Dr. Serena has counseled you to live in the present moment."

I sighed. "Constantly. I can't seem to make it stick."

Kailani threw her arms wide with a smile. "Look around us… sunshine, ocean, and even trade winds. It feels amazing!"

I had to laugh at her spontaneous exuberance. I wish I was made that way, but lasting happiness still felt elusive. It seemed I was always trying to guard against an uncertain future by having low expectations—better to be disappointed than to be crushed when your dreams didn't come true.

"Happiness is a *choice,* and Aunt Lily was always a cup half empty type. And… you don't have to go to the memorial. You can honor Ginnie in another way or ask Rodrigo to go with you… I bet he'd be willing to support you. Afterall, Ginnie was like a mother to you. He'd understand."

"You make it sound so easy. I wish I could be more like you!"

Kailani laughed. "I had many dark nights of the soul, *sista.* You think it was easy coming out to my family?" She shook her head. "I had to decide it was important to be real with them. I was scared shitless!"

"How'd you do it?"

"I was so tired of being fake and scared that I'd be found out. It was a fuck it moment. Some liquid courage helped, too!"

We heard some splashing from the cove, and Kailani and I peered over the rocky cliff to see a turtle splashing around.

"I don't think that's Lono," Kailani said.

"Really?"

"Is it Lono's energy? Sharks have strong electromagnetic sensors. Each of us has a unique energy signature. That's how I can sense when you're nearby. I just tune into you."

Kailani was always dialed in and seemed like an expert at everything.

"I don't know how to do that."

"Don't worry… you just need some practice. I grew up learning how from my grandmother and Nakoa."

"The *Egg Man?*"

She laughed. "Yes… *him.* He's a gifted teacher and healer."

Once again, I envied the nurturing and supportive home that Kailani had been brought up in. Her unique paranormal gifts had been nurtured and honored by her grandmother. I realized this was often the root of my unhappiness—I always felt like the quirky outsider. It seemed everyone else had that joyful, Norman Rockwell-type family *except* me.

"I bet Nakoa would be happy to mentor you."

"I hardly know him. I'd be too embarrassed to ask."

"I'll put in a good word for you."

"What does he charge?"

Kailani shook her head. "He doesn't charge. He wants to preserve his legacy and pass on his wisdom. You'd be perfect—he could teach you how to summon turtles."

"That would be cool to learn."

We heard a car honking from the parking lot and turned to see Rodrigo in the lodge van waving at us. I gestured for him to come over. He slowly edged the van near us and rolled down his window.

"*Howzit?*"

It still amazed me how quickly he'd adapted to pidgin English. Even stranger was hearing him speak it.

Kailani went over to the van window and they bumped fists. "We should get some breakfast. I'm *starved*!" she said.

"Yeah, Sista, let's get some *grinds*," Rodrigo said.

"I'm in," I said.

I hopped into the passenger side. Rodrigo leaned over and kissed me. Kailani opened the side door and quickly climbed in.

"Stop making googly eyes at your man. Let's go!" she said.

"Yes ma'am!" I replied.

Rodrigo hit the gas, and the laughter of my two nearest and dearest companions filled the van.

Baby steps. I don't need to figure out this mano thing right now. I just had to somehow tell Rodrigo. Everything would work itself out.

Chapter Three

My day started with being attacked by a feral rooster. I was wiping down the long, koa-wood dining table on the patio with a damp dishrag when a loud squawk startled me. Frantic flapping wings blinded me, followed by a series of loud, agitated clucks as the bird hopped on my head and pecked at my scalp. I swatted at my hair to ward off the avian attack. This was followed by a series of quick, sharp pecks on my neck and back

"Go away, you little shit!"

Kailani yelled behind me. "Get out!" she shouted.

I looked up to see her furiously brandishing a broom. The bird assailant took off with protesting clucks into the bushes.

"What the hell!" I said.

"You okay?"

Kailani put down the broom.

"I'm fine… a few pecks on my back but nothing major. Thanks."

"Attack of the killer rooster!" she joked. "Let me look."

I pulled down the straps of my cotton tank top. Kailani gently probed my back with her fingertips. Her cool touch was light and gentle.

"You should put something on your back. There's some scratches. Let me get some of Shara's ointments."

I waved her concern away. "I'll have Rodrigo put some calendula ointment on. I'm sure I'll live."

"Lunch service will start soon, I could use some help. Why don't you take care of this first?"

I rolled my eyes. "Yes, Mother!"

She gave me a playful shove. "Go on."

I shook my head but handed her the dishrag and walked back toward the cabin, imagining Rodrigo's amusement when I told him. The air was thick and steamy after the usual morning rain, and I considered jumping into the outdoor shower and a change of clothes. Already my cotton tank top and yoga pants were starting to stick to my skin. I wiped a sheen of perspiration from my forehead with the back of my hand. As I got near to our cabin, I heard Rodrigo's exasperated voice.

"Yeah, Mom, I got it." I hesitated at the front door. "I'm fine and so is Noelani, we don't need any help. Keep your money, we can afford to pay for the wedding. Look, Mom, I gotta run, okay?"

When he ended the call, I opened the front door and stuck my head in.

"Everything okay?" I asked.

He sighed heavily. "Trying to butt in… per usual." He sat at the modest dining table clad only in gray camouflage long board shorts. He forked his fingers through his wavy hair and shook his head in annoyance. "I'm ready to elope!" he declared.

"Really?" I liked the idea of a simple wedding and eloping. My shoulders relaxed as I let out a soft breath.

"No."

"Eloping would be a lot easier than dealing with a wedding planner, a venue, and…."

"You sound like you don't want to do this."

"*I do.* I want to get married. It's just that if we eloped, it'd be less stressful and costly. It'll be just us!"

"I'm having fun with it. I told you I'd be the de facto wedding planner. Shara said she would help too. You don't seem too excited."

"I got attacked by a feral rooster."

"Are you *serious?*" He pushed back from the table and hurried to my side. I pointed at my back. "Jesus. There's scratches and welts. Where is that little shit… I'm going to have him roasted."

"I'm fine." I sighed, pulled off my tank top, and headed to the kitchen cabinet to get the first aid kit. I found a tube of calendula ointment inside and handed it to him. He uncapped the tube and squeezed out a dollop into his palm, then gingerly dabbed my upper back.

"What the hell, these are nasty. I'm going to hunt down the little fucker."

"Don't bother. He's literally flown the coop. What did your mother want?"

"She wants to give us money toward the wedding."

"*And?*"

"All my life, she's tried to buy me off with money. It's her lame way of making up for being a crappy parent. I was shunted off from relative to relative while she gallivanted from self-help workshops to quack psychics who communicated with spirits and did tarot card readings. Don't get me started."

"Sorry. It must have been tough growing up like that."

"It was either psychics or obsessing with meeting her soulmate. I remember waking up from a scary dream when I was about five and running into her bedroom. There was this guy in bed with her— I thought it was my dad. I thought they'd gotten back together. It just turned out to be one of her random hookups."

I slipped my tank top back on and hugged him. "I'm sure she means well by helping out with the wedding costs."

He shrugged. "*Maybe.* So, Shara said you're going to your ex-mother-in-law's memorial?"

I froze. "She did?"

"I guess she thought I knew. She mentioned it after dinner last night—said we could stay at her parent's place in Hawaii Kai."

"I was going to tell you," I blurted.

He pulled back and looked into my eyes. "You don't have to hide things from me. I'm not going to freak out. It's not a big deal."

A wave of relief swept over me and I let out a shaky breath. "Would you come with me?"

"If that's what you want, I'd be happy to."

"Dr. Serena will be here to officiate. We can firm up our wedding plans with her."

"I like Dr. Serena. Is there something else on your mind? If you're having second thoughts… we can put the wedding off."

Rodrigo looked worried—he scrunched his eyebrows and frowned. His directness startled me, and a bubble of anxiety welled up in my chest. My bra straps seemed too tight. *If he thinks his mother is an airy fairy nutjob, what would he think about me being a shapeshifter?* Rodrigo's serious, penetrating stare made my mouth go dry, and my pulse raced nervously.

"Kailani thinks I should study native culture with Nakoa," I blurted.

"Okay. That's what you've been brooding about?"

"Well, some people would think studying with a local shaman could be sketchy. I mean, he doesn't have any actual credentials."

Rodrigo sat down at the table and rubbed his chin.

"Look, learning about your heritage from an Indigenous elder is one thing. Spending hard earned money on tarot card readers is sketchy. So, you're going to study with Nakoa? I think that's great."

"It's not just history lessons, he's also a respected healer."

"When do you start your shaman training?"

"I haven't actually spoken to him yet… he might say no."

"I doubt that. I can't believe you've been stressing about Nakoa. I'm not like your ex-husband. I actually care about your well-being."

"I'm glad to hear that."

Rodrigo shook his head. "You worry about the strangest things."

A jab of guilt poked me. *I should just tell him right now. Why prolong this?*

"Are you sure that's all?" Rodrigo asked.

I nodded. "I better go help with lunch service."

"Hey, will you look at those wedding cake links I sent you when you get back?"

"Sure. We'll go through them together."

I headed to the front door as Rodrigo caught my wrist. "I love you."

I smiled. "I love you too."

I slipped out the door and put on my sandals. A sense of foreboding fanned over me. *I'll tell him soon.* I promised myself...
I had to.

Chapter Four

After a hearty lunch of *loco moco* at our favorite diner in Hilo, Rodrigo and I came back to the lodge. It was our day off since we both worked on the weekends when the inn was busiest. It was so nice to have a lazy day with no plans. The humid day made me drowsy, and I begged off going for our usual mid-day walk. With a suggestive smile, I suggested a cuddle session, which he instantly agreed to. We curled up spoon-style as the ceiling fan churned lazily above the bed. I enjoyed the musky scent of patchouli soap wafting off his skin.

"You smell amazing," I murmured.

"You taste amazing," he replied and playfully nipped my earlobe. A feeling of soothing calm enveloped us as we drifted off.

An annoying scratching sound jostled me awake. I reached for Rodrigo, but he was gone. I sat up and stared groggily at the empty, rumpled spot next to me. *Where is he?* I quickly realized the irritating noise was Ozzie, the wiener dog, scratching at the front door.

"*Ozzie!*" I hissed, climbing out of bed and pushing the door open. Ozzie looked up at me and barked sharply. "You are a pain in the butt!" I said.

He circled me once and gave me an imploring look.

"Out!" I said.

I heard a notification beep from my phone and went over to the nightstand. There was a text from Rodrigo. *Sorry, babe, Shara came by and asked if I'd help her load the garbage into the lodge van. Since I was up, I decided I might as well drive her to the transfer station. I'll be back quickly... promise.*

I groaned inwardly. It felt like we were constantly interrupted anytime we had some private time to ourselves. In the beginning, I was happy he liked to pitch in, but now, a sting of resentment bristled inside me.

Ozzie raced back into the cabin with an insistent bark. I looked down at him as he spun around in a frantic circle, then ran off. I groaned again and slipped on my sandals. *What the hell is going on with him?* I followed him down the narrow, gravel path toward the yoga yurt. The front door was propped open with a bright-red bromeliad plant in a terracotta clay pot. Ozzie nimbly ran up the short, wooden stairs and rushed inside. Despite the door being partially open, the heat inside was intense. It was like walking into a dry sauna and was hard to breathe. The lights were off, and in the dim lighting, I saw someone lying near the altar on a yoga mat. He was tall and slender, dressed all in white cotton—a long tunic and loose yoga pants. I guessed he was in his early thirties, with long, light-brown hair and a neatly trimmed goatee. Ozzie ran right up to him and pawed at him.

"Ozzie!"

My scalp prickled, and an uneasy sensation swept over me, my gut clenching. Something was wrong. I moved closer and looked down. He was breathing in shallow gasps. As I leaned over him, his eyes fluttered open briefly, and I looked into ocean blue eyes.

"Hey, Gorgeous," he murmured.

Before I could respond, his eyes shut, and he became still. *Something is definitely wrong.* I remembered when Jason and I were hiking in Lake Tahoe one summer, he became seriously dehydrated. He had gotten unusually sweaty and disoriented. I'd brought along a canteen of water, but he had insisted I drink it all. When we got back to the parking lot, I had to rush him to an urgent care clinic, where he got hooked up to an IV machine. I looked around the yurt and saw the large, glass, water dispenser filled with filtered water and cucumber slices near the entrance. The dispenser was completely full. There was a set of unused ceramic lodge mugs next to it. I quickly filled a mug and went back to the inert man. *Is this Braydon?* I set the mug down and leaned over him. A strong scent of roses floated off him.

"Braydon?" I whispered.

"Uh huh," he murmured.

Under any other circumstance, I'd have laughed, but I was unsure how to proceed. I debated how to get him to sit up.

"Can you sit up, Braydon? I've got some water for you."

His eyes remained shut. I thought about running over to the lodge to get Kailani. She was always levelheaded and calm in a crisis. Then I heard a familiar voice at the door.

"*Aunty!* What's going on?"

I looked up to see Lono standing at the entrance.

"I found him like this. I think he's got heat stroke, or maybe he's dehydrated."

Lono came over quickly and knelt down. "It's Braydon." The new yoga teacher.

Lono slipped his arm around Braydon's shoulders and helped him to sit up. I handed Lono the mug.

"Hey, *bro*. Easy does it." He lifted the mug to Braydon's lips, and I went back to the water dispenser. There was a cotton dishrag on top. I dampened the dishrag with cucumber water and went back to Braydon, gently dabbing his face.

Braydon's eyes fluttered open, and he stared at us dazedly.

"*Drink*," Lono urged.

Braydon took a few dainty sips of water.

"Good," he said.

"I think Shara keeps Pedialyte at the lodge," I said.

"We should take him to urgent care," Lono replied. We sat quietly as Braydon took a few more sips of water.

"I'm good," he said.

Lono shook his head. "I think it's best we take you to urgent care."

Braydon slowly started to get up but collapsed against him.

"Can you get my truck and pull up next to the yurt?" Lono said. "Be right back."

I hurried out of the yurt and down the short steps toward the main lodge. As I rushed along the narrow path toward the lodge, I found Lono's black truck parked in front of the main building. I yanked the door open and was relieved to see the keys in the ignition. I started the engine and turned the truck back toward the yurt. As I got closer, Lono tottered out gingerly, supporting Braydon with his arm around his waist as they came down the steps. I jumped out and opened the passenger door as Lono helped Braydon get into the truck. I hovered anxiously as Lono got into the truck cab.

"Should I go with you?"

Lono shook his head. "Let Shara and Kailani know what's going on. I'll text you."

I stood back as he pulled away from the yurt and sped off. I went inside to get some water to refresh myself, filling an empty mug with cucumber water and slurping it down. I hadn't realize how parched I was. I noticed a small, shiny object on the floor next to the altar and went over, spotting a small, gold hoop earring. *Braydon's?* I picked it up and felt a strange tingling in my palm—a vision flashed before me. I saw Braydon standing alone on a beach, waving with a smile. "Until we meet again!" he said.

What the hell was that?

Suddenly, Ozzie shot through the open door and began pawing at my bare legs. He was followed by Diana, who stood in the doorway with her balled fists on her hips.

"I've been chasing that little mongrel around for the last thirty minutes!" she declared. She moved into the yurt and scooped a wriggling Ozzie into her arms. She was dressed in an oversized, men's cotton t-shirt, with the lodge logo across her ample bosom. Black leggings with matching black Croc sandals completed her casual attire.

"Why do you have to stress out Kailani, you little *shit*?" she said, cradling Ozzie in her arms.

"You missed the drama," I said.

Diana looked up at me. "I saw Lono driving away like a bat outta hell. You mean *that*?"

I nodded. "Have you met Braydon yet? I found him passed out in here… or rather… Ozzie alerted me."

Ozzie let out a sharp bark at his name, and Diana chuckled.

"Okay, Ozzie, you're the hero," I admitted, then gestured at the round, cotton meditation pillows. "I'm going to sit and sip some water. I seem to always forget to drink enough." I took a sip of the refreshing cucumber water and lowered myself onto the pillow, cross-legged. I explained what happened to Braydon as Diana remained standing, gently stroking Ozzie's head affectionately.

"When did you get back from California?" I asked.

"Last night."

"You were gone for a while… like a month, right?"

"Closer to three weeks, but it's nice to be back. We need to catch up. How's it going with you and lover boy?"

"We're fine."

"Let me see that rock he gave you."

I extended my left hand, and Diana bent over my ring finger to admire the diamond, emerald, and pearl engagement ring.

"He spent some bucks on that," she said.

"I told him not to go overboard!" I glanced down at the one carat, pear-shaped diamond flanked by a dainty, rectangular emerald and akoya pearl on each side, set in yellow gold. The emerald represented Rodrigo's Taurus sign, and the pearl represented my Cancer sign.

"You excited… the date's gonna be here before you know it."

I shrugged. "I already had the big, fancy wedding. I'd rather just elope or keep it small. But… he really wants a wedding."

"A lot of women would love to have your problem. Devoted, sexy, younger man who would walk on hot coals for you. I'm jealous!"

"I thought we'd have a long engagement, but he wants to get married before he turns forty." I sighed.

"Forty seems so young from where I stand," Diana said.

"Right? He's got the stamina of a teenager."

"I bet he's great in bed."

"He's more talented than my *wusband*," I joked.

"Now I'm *really* jealous."

I pulled my knees up and avoided Diana's gaze. Acquaintances always seemed to think I always had it easy—first being married to an acclaimed restaurant owner and now being with a handsome, younger man. Even my normally reserved probate attorney congratulated me on so quickly landing on my feet.

"Life is so easy when you're young and pretty," he'd said.

"I was a high school *nerd,*" I had retorted. "I wasn't popular at all," I added as I left his office. The memory made me cringe inwardly.

"I know it seems like I have the perfect life with Rodrigo, but it's not always rainbows and unicorns every day," I said.

"Hey, I'd trade places with you in a heartbeat!"

A bubble of frustration percolated in my chest, which was followed by a jab of guilt. *I do have it good—I have a man who's madly in love with me.* Yet I had also suffered through a horrible divorce and betrayal. My cheeks reddened at the memory of Jason's dishonesty and infidelity. Not to mention the humiliation I experienced when it was obvious to his restaurant staff what was going on.

Diana leaned over and put her hand on my shoulder. "I remember the gory details about your divorce. If it was my ex-husband who had taken that money from me, I'd have hunted him down and cut off his nuts!" Diana let out a hearty laugh. "You handled it with dignity and class. I admire that about you."

I lifted my shoulders and sighed. "Believe me, I had some murderous revenge fantasies. I just decided he wasn't worth all that effort."

"I'm glad you bounced back from it. You deserve to be happy."

I looked up at Diana. Her voice was gentle, and her soft expression was touching. "I appreciate that. You and Kailani played a big role in keeping me sane."

Ozzie wriggled loose from her and scampered out the door. Diana and I watched him disappear into the jungle.

"There he goes!" Diana sighed. "Just like the men in my life—always on the run!"

I rubbed Diana's back. "Then it's their loss."

Chapter Five

Our second day off with no plans, I made Rodrigo promise to take me to the beach for the day. We also made a pact to totally unplug and leave our cell phones behind. He went ahead to the kitchen to pack us a picnic lunch. After sipping my second cup of coffee, I headed to the lodge to meet him. To my surprise, I saw Braydon cleaning the windows of the lodge van with a microfiber cloth. He was dressed in orange board shorts with brightly colored starfish, flip flops, and retro, round, orange sunglasses that complemented his swim trunks. His hair was styled in a modern mullet, with his thick, wavy, light-brown hair full on top and the sides shaved close.

"Hey you!" Braydon called out. He put down the cloth and rushed toward me, enveloping me in a warm hug.

"Whoa…!" I said and took a step back from him. My skin tingled, and a wooziness swept through me. It was like I'd swallowed a glass of champagne. I saw a golden halo of light with sparkles around his head, like someone threw face glitter at him.

Braydon gave me a funny look. "What's the matter?" he asked.

"Nothing. You're kind of glowing!"

What is going on? It was a strange feeling.

He chuckled. "I do have an exceptionally bright aura. By the way, thanks for saving my life," Braydon said.

"Ozzie deserves all the credit. How're you feeling?"

"I'm good. Stupid me letting myself get dehydrated like that."

"It happens. I'm just glad you're okay—you look pretty good."

Braydon's appearance was a sharp contrast from the day at the yurt. His skin glowed with a healthy rosiness, and his blue eyes sparkled with vitality.

"I heard you two are headed to Kuko Beach. I love that place. I used to body surf there back in the day."

"You did? When was that?"

He shrugged with a sly smile. "Back in Lemurian times."

"Oh really?" I raised my eyebrows. *He must be joking, right?*

"If you listen carefully, you can hear Namaka calling to you at Kuko Beach."

"Namaka… Pele's ocean sister?"

He nodded. "Namaka is a hard one to resist. I can feel her presence at Kuko Beach. She calls to me like a sultry sea siren!" he joked.

"I don't know much about Namaka."

"Girl, talk about family drama. Pele stole Namaka's husband and *ooooooof*—the shit hit the fan. Even their shark brother, *Kamohoali'i* got involved. Namaka won that battle because she's a total bad ass."

"But didn't Pele ultimately prevail because she fled to Mauna Loa—her sacred resting place?"

Braydon nodded with a smile. "That's right. So, where's your sexy fiancé?"

I nodded toward the lodge kitchen. "Rodridgo's getting our picnic lunch."

"Kailani told me all about your dreamy courtship."

"She did?"

"And your asshat of an ex-husband. *Girl,* you definitely upgraded!"

Before I could respond, the loud thud of the lodge kitchen door banging shut caught my attention. I looked over to see Rodrigo emerge with a big, wicker picnic basket. Braydon shot Rodrigo an appreciative side eye. My cheeks burned with embarrassment. Braydon grinned and mimed zipping his lips and tossing the key over his shoulder. "Your secrets are safe with me, babe," he whispered. Rodrigo came up beside me and slipped an arm around my shoulders.

"Shara hooked us up. Grilled tofu sandwiches, taro chips, fruit salad, and iced tea."

"This is Braydon, the new yoga instructor!" I said.

"Aloha, Bryadon. How're you feeling?"

Braydon rolled his eyes. "I guess everybody's heard about me fainting."

"Happens to the best of us," Rodrigo said. "What's up? What're you two chatting about?"

"Oh, nothing—just how we make a good couple," I said quickly.

At the same time, Braydon said, "How adorable you two are and her asshat ex-husband."

"Her ex-husband was an asshat." Rodrigo replied. My face reddened again. "It was bad enough he openly cheated on her but to take her money like that? Like I said... *asshat.*" Rodrigo shook his head in disgust.

"We'd better head out," I said quickly antsy to get going before Rodrigo got roped into helping out with something at the last minute.

"Nice meeting you," Rodrigo said.

"I might catch you guys later. I was going to head that way after my class this morning."

"Great. We'll see you later, then," I said.

Braydon waved at me as I climbed into the lodge van. Rodrigo put the picnic basket on the back seat. When he climbed into the driver's seat, he leaned over and squeezed my knee affectionately.

"What a character!" he said.

"You don't even know the half of it."

Like… *when he used to live in Lemuria?*

***

Kuko Beach was a twenty minute drive away. I rolled down the passenger side window and relished the cool air blowing on my face.

"I like that guy, Braydon," Rodrigo said.

"It's only because he said you were an upgrade."

He grinned. "Yeah, there's *that*."

"I can't believe Kailani shared my divorce details."

"I'm sure it wasn't that. You know how Kailani is… she was probably being chatty. Besides, you posted about your divorce on Facebook, so it's not like a big secret."

"I only posted a couple things… when I finally got the divorce papers back. It was a celebration. I'm not like Cassie, posting every hour."

"Let it go… you're overthinking this."

I started to react but changed my mind. We were finally going to spend a carefree day together with no plans. I didn't want to ruin the moment.

***

There was no traffic on the wide, paved road, and we got to Kuko Beach quickly. Rodrigo and I trekked slowly down the sloped, narrow, single track through dense, jungle foliage. We gingerly tiptoed over the rocky, black beach to avoid getting cut by the sharp stones. Unlike the alabaster, fine sands on Waikiki beaches, Kuko beach was all rugged terrain with dramatic cliffs. We heard the thunderous roar of waves slamming against the cliffs as we approached the cove. At the end of the trail, the vista opened to a sun-dappled, pristine cove.

"Is this for real?" Rodrigo sighed.

We took in the aquamarine water and foamy, white-tipped waves crashing against the large, black, lava boulders encircling the cove. I grabbed Rodrigo's hand, and we stepped carefully over smaller basalt stones embedded in the beach. I put down a camp pad and thick, striped beach blanket near the water, then plopped down. Rodrigo put down the large picnic basket and sat down next to me. I stripped off my hoodie and denim shorts to reveal my two piece swimsuit and reached for the small glass bottle of herbal suntan lotion.

Rodrigo grimaced. "Are you sure that's going to work?"

"I trust Shara. She researches everything fully."

I removed the top and poured some onto my palm. "It smells good and is reef safe."

Rodrigo leaned over and sniffed. "Yeah, okay, but will it protect you?"

I shrugged and massaged the lotion on my arms and legs. The delicate scent of neroli and lavender was pleasant. "I'd trust Shara's expertise over all the chemicals in regular sunscreen," I replied.

Rodrigo sighed and took off his lodge t-shirt. "I'd like to believe in being organic and all natural, but…"

"But… *what*?"

"I mean, I applaud Shara and Kailani, trying to create an eco paradise, but it's just not practical and sustainable."

"Why not?" I continued to rub lotion on my belly.

"It's like a drop in the ocean." He waved his arm in an arc toward the water. "It's nice messaging, but everyone has to get on board to make it worthwhile."

"I think we have to set an example. The sunscreen has been a best seller at the lodge store and online. People want to be healthier and protect the environment."

"I get that. But think about the bigger issues like when all that military jet fuel spilled into the drinking water on Oahu. *That* was a big deal."

I nodded. "That *was* a big deal. I'm just saying, small efforts can make a big impact overall."

Rodrigo leaned back on his elbows and stared out at the waves. "Such a beautiful, magical place. I guess you're right… we have to start somewhere."

We reclined on our beach towels contentedly, soaking up the sun. It was so good to just relax and do nothing. I dozed off for a few minutes.

After a while, Rodrigo gently poked me and said, "Let's go for a dip, my beautiful nature girl."

I got up as he held out his hand.

He grabbed my hand and pulled me toward him for a light kiss.

We made our way toward the tidepools. The water was remarkably clear and swirled and gurgled around the sharp rocks. I dipped my toes, then my feet into the water and waded out into the ocean until I was waist deep. Rodrigo waded up alongside me and wrapped his arms around my waist. We bobbed together, enjoying the cool, salty waves washing over us. I self-consciously grazed my fingertips along the sides of my neck, worried that my gills would pop out. To my relief, my skin was smooth and firm.

Time always seemed to slip away at the beach. The sun dipped lower on the horizon, the wind picked up, and the waves got choppier. Rodrigo gestured to swim ashore. I dog-paddled toward the beach and got out. We went back to our picnic spot and retrieved our beach towels. After we patted ourselves somewhat dry, we sat down. Rodrigo took out the bag of taro chips and fruit salad, biting hungrily into a tofu sandwich.

"I wish this was a big, greasy cheeseburger," he sighed wistfully.

"We can stop somewhere on the way back," I said.

He shrugged. "God forbid Shara smell animal meat off us. Sometimes there are too many rules… no plastic, no GMO food, no meat, no smoking or drinking…"

"I thought you liked that part?"

"I do… it's wholesome and all that."

"They're just doing their bit to curb microplastic pollution. Statistically, we all consume like a credit card size of microplastics every year." I shuddered.

"I get that, but it's too much. Luckily, it's just for a year."

"What do you mean?"

"We made an agreement we'd try it for a year."

"We did? I don't remember that."

"You said… '*Let's try it for a year and then commit.*' Seriously, you don't remember that?"

"You don't like it here? You acted excited to come here and be part of the community."

"Of course I like it… *for now*. But I'm not making any money. I gave up my job to come here with you." Rodrigo grimaced and crumbled up his sandwich wrapper. "Shara got on my case about separating the recycling correctly. I mean… *really?*"

"They love having you here—Kailani even told me the other day how much she appreciates you helping out in the garden and doing garbage runs to the transfer station. I can't imagine Shara criticizing you."

"She said it nicely, but I guess I accidentally tossed in a black plastic take out box." He sighed. "So… lesson learned. No plastic utensils, no black take-out boxes, no Styrofoam take-out boxes."

"Sorry. I'm sure she meant well. Is there something else going on?"

"I've been getting job offers in California. The pay is really good… I could run my own physical therapy clinic."

I took in what he disclosed silently, surprised at our disconnect. *Hadn't I made it clear that I wanted to stay in my happy place indefinitely?*

"I mean, is this life what you imagined for us for the long term?" Rodrigo asked.

My shoulders slumped as I shook my head. A jab of shame stirred in my gut. My aunt's scowling face popped into my head. *"Always thinking of yourself. Such a selfish child!"*

"I guess I didn't really think it through—sorry."

"Hey." Rodrigo leaned over and put his hand over mine. "There's nothing to be sorry for. I get it… this is your happy place. Besides, I was going to wait and bring it up after the wedding. I mean, we've been here nine months already."

Nine months! It felt like we'd just arrived.

"We can always come back," Rodrigo added.

"You sound like you've made up your mind already," I sighed. My throat tightened. My dream of living *forever after* on the islands was quickly dissolving. I blinked back tears.

"We have the same goal. We want to build a life together, and that means having the funds to do that. These opportunities happen to be back in California… *for now.*"

I smiled wanly. "I guess you're right."

"Let's just enjoy the moment, okay? Hey… *look!*"

I turned to look where Rodrigo was pointing and saw two Spinner dolphins leap out of the water side-by-side. Goddess Namaka had blessed us with a special omen.

Chapter Six

I heard Nakoa and Kailani on the lanai laughing easily as they enjoyed their mango smoothies.

I just have to ask Nakoa if I can study with him… what's the big deal? What's the worst thing that can happen—he says no, right?

I tried to ignore the nervous fluttering in my stomach. My mind whirred through different hypothetical scenarios. I knew I was being silly and wished I'd asked Kailani to help me. *Ugh.*

The refreshing, fragrant scent of strawberries wafted through the kitchen. I busied myself with carefully slicing the berries for the fruit salad on the lunch menu. It was still morning, and cooling breezes swept pleasantly through the room. By lunch, the humidity would be stifling, and even having two churning ceiling fans wouldn't make a difference.

The kitchen door squeaked open. I turned to see Nakoa standing in the doorway, smiling at me.

"Kailani said there's a fresh batch of plantation tea in the 'fridge?"

"Let me get that for you." I wiped my hands on a damp dishrag on the counter and I reached for a tall water glass on the dish rack.

As I opened the refrigerator door, Nakoa stepped into the kitchen. "So, I hear you're interested in studying with me?"

My stomach flip flopped nervously. I pulled the iced tea pitcher out of the refrigerator and poured some into the glass.

"Um… yes! I mean, if you have time? If you're too busy…"

"I haven't had a student in a long time. I think it's time to start again."

I turned away from the counter and handed him the iced tea. His brilliant smile lit up his face. He had kind eyes that crinkled attractively in the corners. He must have been quite a ladies man in his younger days.

"Great! I wasn't sure if you were taking on protégés."

"I think you'd be an excellent student."

A sense of relief swept through me, and a lightness enveloped me as I smiled at Nakoa. "Really? Why is that?"

He shrugged. "Kailani speaks highly of you. Also, I haven't a changeling student in some time. This could be quite interesting."

My cheeks got hot. "What does *that* mean?"

He shook his head at my expression. "Nothing to worry about. I think we could learn a lot from each other."

My mouth fell open unexpectedly. "Kailani told you about my mano self?"

He laughed. "No, I already sensed it when we first met. What are you doing tonight? We can start right away."

Tonight? I wasn't ready for that. My mouth went dry as I leaned into the kitchen counter.

He chuckled. "We can wait if that's too soon."

"No, it's fine. I don't have any plans."

"I'll meet you inside the yoga yurt after dinner."

Nakoa went back to the lanai. As I watched him depart, my stomach knotted up uncomfortably. *What did I just commit to?*

＊＊＊

The stillness inside the yurt was relaxing. Adding to the tranquil moment was the scent of jasmine flowers blooming outside and the softly lit room. Tall, cream-colored pillar candles on the wooden altar provided ambient light. We sat cross-legged opposite each other on round meditation pillows.

"Let's take a few breaths together," Nakoa said.

I followed his lead,, and we inhaled deeply three times. He then bowed his head and murmured a brief prayer. When I opened my eyes he passed over a set of Zener cards. The cards depicted five symbols: a circle, a cross, a square, a star, and three wavy lines. Then he turned the deck facedown so the symbols were hidden. Beside Nakoa was also a stack of plain white envelopes and a plastic clipboard with a pen.

"This is a warm-up. Tune into each card and flip one over. Focus on the initial *shape*. Is it a straight line? Is it a curved line?"

My palms were moist with anxiety. My mouth was arid and my heart thudded nervously. I hadn't felt this tense since high school finals.

Focus!

As I flipped over each card, my shoulders sagged with defeat. I got them all wrong, even after three tries. I wanted to sink into the floor. *How could I not get even one right?*

Nakoa leaned over and patted my hand. "Just tell me straight or curved."

That didn't work either.

"Why don't we take a break?"

I sighed and got up. To complicate matters, I knew Rodrigo was going to walk over to pick me up. We had planned to go to the lodge kitchen after my session to get dessert. I had cautioned him that it might be longer than an hour, yet he had shrugged it off.

I went to the ceramic water dispenser and helped myself to a mug of cucumber water. *How can I be so bad at this?* It brought up humiliating memories of trying out for different high school sports, only to be rejected. I gulped down the water and savored the fresh taste of cucumber. I also remembered how Dr. Serena always told me to recall a happy memory whenever I felt like a failure. So, I thought about the time Kailani and I had shaved ice near Waikiki. Then I put my hand over my belly and whispered, "All is well in this moment." A lightness rippled over me. I refilled the mug with water and took another generous swig. Behind me, Nakoa laughed and clapped his hands.

"You *are* picking the right cards. You're jumping ahead."

I turned and looked at him in confusion. He shuffled the cards and handed them back to me. "Try again."

I put the mug down next to the water dispenser and sat back down. He waved at the stack of cards, and I took a deep breath.

"Straight line… square?"

I flipped it over and it was a triangle. *I was getting closer!*

"The next one." Nakoa said. "It's a *square.*"

He was right. My chest swelled with happiness. The next round, I got better. Nakoa grinned broadly.

"You see? Let's move on and try something different." He reached over and picked up a white envelope, handing it to me. "Place this on your forehead and tune into the image inside." He passed over the clipboard and instructed me to start sketching what

I perceived in my mind's eye. There was also a questionnaire I was supposed to complete. It had questions like:

- Note colors you see
- Note the following: smell/temperature/text/sounds
- Perception

"Relax and start drawing. Don't think," Nakoa murmured.

Don't think... right! I began to sketch, and an image began to form of a bicycle. *It's a blue bicycle.* The smell is clean, the temperature is warm, there is no text, and it's quiet inside the scene. I saw a long, bright hallway. I wrote, *college dormitory?* I put my pen down and looked up expectantly at Nakoa. He smiled as I passed the envelope to him. He opened the envelope, and his smile broadened.

"Would you like to see?" he teased. He passed the picture to me. My mouth fell open as I studied it. The scene was a blue wheelchair inside a long, narrow hallway. It looked like a hospital setting with bright, overhead lights.

"You see? When you relax, it's easy. I give you an A+!" he joked.

I released a loud exhale and laughed.

I did it. I can't believe it!

Nakoa leaned toward me and patted my shoulder. "Remember… the magic only works if you're in a relaxed state."

I thought about the wheelchair, and a ripple of happiness fanned through me. *I did good!*

"I think you've earned your dessert. I believe Shara made a banana cream pie."

We both stood together, and I impulsively hugged Nakoa. His arms were surprisingly toned and firm.

"Thank you, Nakoa."

He bowed his head. "Thank you for agreeing to be my student."

I hurried over to the yurt door and opened it to see Rodrigo walking toward me.

"I'm done!" I sang out.

He looked up and smiled. "Yeah? What cosmic secrets did Nakoa impart?"

"No secrets. C'mon… let's get to the kitchen."

Rodrigo took my hand. "So, what happened?"

"I'll tell you along the way."

We moved down the path, which was lit with bronze, solar lanterns. We were accompanied by the nighttime chirping of coqui frogs. I described my session with Nakoa excitedly. When I finished, we'd arrived at the lodge kitchen. I looked at Rodrigo. "Isn't that cool?" I asked.

Rodrigo spread his hands out. "Sure."

"I have a superpower," I joked.

"Looking at playing cards? You're starting to sound like my mother."

"I'm not your mother."

"I know that. I didn't say you were."

I threw up my hands. "You prided yourself on being a decent softball pitcher. You said you spent hours learning how to throw a fastball. It's a talent you had that you took pride in. It's like… *that*."

"I don't see how you can possibly make that connection."

"Unlike you, I was never good at anything. I scraped by in high school. My grades were average."

"We were all like that."

"Not you. You said you were the president of the science club and won softball awards. You scored ridiculously high on the SAT test."

He shrugged. "I got lucky on the SAT test. Those activities were my way to cope with my crazy parents."

"I want to explore my heritage."

"Your *heritage?*"

A jolt of fear shot through me. I wasn't ready to disclose my changeling self yet. *Holy shit…now what?*

"You mean your Hawaiian heritage?"

I nodded quickly. "*Exactly.*"

"Okay… you could have told me that."

I opened the kitchen door and stepped into the stuffy kitchen. The delicious, sugary smell of baked goods was soothing. I opened the refrigerator and saw a covered glass pie dish. I turned and carefully placed the pie on the counter, then removed the foil covering the top.

"Let's take these back to the cabin. We have a big day tomorrow."

I shrugged. "It doesn't matter to me."

Rodrigo went in search of paper take-out boxes. He returned a few minutes later with a box, and I carefully inserted two pieces of pie, then re-wrapped the pie and put the dish back in the refrigerator. We slipped back out into the night.

"Are you ready to see Jason again?" Rodrigo asked.

I shook my head. "I had no plans to ever see him again."

"You don't have to go. If we bail right now, no one's going to care."

"I know."

We walked silently. *Maybe I should just bail on this. I don't owe Jason anything. That part of my life is over, and Ginny's recent passing was the final chapter.*

"I don't really want to go, but Ginny was like a mother to me. I want to honor her."

"Okay." Rodrigo slipped his arm around my shoulders. "You're a good person," he said.

"So are you."

We reached the cabin, our home. This was my *tabula rasa,* and tomorrow was a final goodbye.

Chapter Seven

The Hilo airport was small and quaint compared to the other island airports. It lacked the busyness and bustling energy common to airports in general, and that suited me. Rodrigo and I sat comfortably in one of the large sofas arranged in a U shape in the lobby. Behind us was a small gift store and a coffee stand. He seemed like he was in a good mood as he sat slouched against the thick cloth seat cushions with his legs stretched out.

He reached over and patted my knee. "You feeling nervous about the memorial tomorrow?"

"Why should I… you'll be there."

He raised his eyebrows. "Jason better behave, is all I'm saying."

"There'll be lots of people around, including Dr. Serena."

"I'm sure he'll be thinking impure thoughts about you."

I hadn't confided in Rodrigo about that disastrous night in Jason's hotel room. I still cringed when I thought about how gullible I was. *What was I thinking?* The shock of seeing Candace's pierced nipple still haunted me. *But does he know about me actually hooking up with Jason?* An eddy of anxiety swirled in my belly.

"I remember that Don Henley song you sent me. I felt terrible for avoiding you and running away. I'm sorry."

"I couldn't sleep all night. I thought about you being with him—I was sure you were getting back with him."

A lump formed in my throat at the thought of Rodrigo fretting over me. I blinked back tears.

He put his hand over mine. "I know it was tough on you. You spent twenty years with him. I was just this guy you were hooking up with."

My heart squeezed painfully at his words. First, that he could be so forgiving and secondly that he thought that he was just a meaningless hook up.

"You weren't just a casual hook up—you meant something to me. You always will."

He leaned over and caressed my face. "Thanks for that."

His iPhone chimed, signaling a text. He glanced down and moaned. "Oh, damn."

I glanced up at the sharpness of his tone. "What's wrong?"

"My Mom. She wants to meet up."

"She's *here…* on the Big Island?"

He shook his head glumly. "No on Oahu. I hate it when she springs this shit on me."

He showed the text message to me: *Hi, son… missing you. I'm actually here in Honolulu attending a Lemurian activation ceremony. You mentioned you might be here this week. I know it's last minute, and if you both can't make it… it's fine. Just wanted to reach out. Love, Mom."*

I was puzzled at Rodrigo's reaction. Her message sounded nice.

"A Lemurian activation ceremony? What's that?"

Rodrigo rolled his eyes. "Don't get me started."

"We should meet up… it'd be fun, since the only time we've met is over Zoom calls. Anyway, I'd love to hear about your mother's Lemurian ceremony. I have so many questions!" I teased.

"Don't encourage her… she'll talk your ear off."

I mimicked Margot's voice. *"Son… remember… we're spirits with bodies not bodies with spirits!"*

Rodrigo swatted at me. "Please stop. I grew up listening to that shit."

I laughed at his discomfort. "You don't believe in that… even just a little?

He sighed. "Of course I believe we have souls."

"Does it bother you when Kailani talks about her spiritual heritage? Her great grandmother was a famous healer. She used to heal broken bones by chanting and using herbal poultices. Is that so far-fetched? Or that Kailani and I share a similar spiritual heritage?"

"It wouldn't surprise me."

"Even if I told you I was a shapeshifter too?"

Rodrigo laughed at that. "Come on."

We were interrupted by an announcement that the boarding was commencing at the upstairs gate. We got up, gathered our carry-on bags, and walked over to the escalators. Upstairs, the gate area was compact and small. I looked around and was surprised to see how crowded it was. All the plastic chairs were occupied. Within minutes, several disembarking passengers from the jetway flooded past us. We were ready to board.

***

We were seated in the front rows behind first class on the brief, forty minute interisland happy hop flight. I decided to catch up with Cassie's latest Instagram posts. I hadn't read any of her posts for weeks. I had to admit I didn't enjoy reviewing her perfect life now that she was starting over with her husband and new baby.

Rodrigo stared out the small oval window. Cream colored clouds floated like huge cotton puffs against the periwinkle-blue sky. I handed my phone over to Rodrigo.

"Cassie's perfect life," I said.

He scanned her social media posts briefly and handed my phone back without commenting.

"Cassie always had everything. Back in high school, she was the head cheerleader and even dated the captain of the football team."

"So *cliché*."

"I'm serious. She had rich, doting parents, a convertible VW bug, and the cutest clothes."

"Must be nice."

"The only reason Kailani and I didn't hate her was she was genuinely nice to everyone. She spent her allowance buying us snacks and paying for movies. She took Kailani and me to our first concert at the Warfield Theater in San Francisco. We saw Robert Palmer when he was promoting his Riptide album."

I remembered how grown-up we felt after Cassie's mother dropped us off in front of the iconic theater. Inside the ornate lobby were gilded crystal chandeliers and dark-red velvet seats facing the stage.

"Robert Palmer?"

"You know, "Addicted to Love"?"

Rodrigo shook his head slowly. "When you guys were in high school, I wasn't even born yet."

My cheeks turned red. *"Oh, right."*

"My first concert was Bruno Mars in Berkeley with my dad. He was thrilled to see a brown man live on stage. It was really cool. I asked this girl to go with me but she stood me up. So, I called my dad, and he rushed over. How pathetic is that… having my father be my date for my first live concert?"

"I think it's sweet."

"I never fit in because the stuck up girls thought my father was a lowly Hispanic auto mechanic, and he drove a Pontiac Firebird Trans Am. All the cool girls' parents drove expensive European cars. Cars that cost more than my dad made in a year."

I reached over and squeezed his hand. "Those girls missed out. They didn't see the diamond in the rough you were… plus being hot and sexy!" I added.

He squeezed my hand back. "I wasn't hot and sexy… I was nerdy. I liked science and math and was a *Star Trek* geek. Plus, it was a depressing time because my parents split up when I started high school. I stayed with my father for a while, but he started drinking to cope with the divorce. It was rough."

"I'm sorry to hear how much you've gone through."

He shrugged. "It's in the rearview mirror."

"You never talk about your father. What happened to him?"

"He died from alcohol poisoning. Literally drank himself to death. He never got over the divorce and my mother's cheating."

"What?"

"Yeah… she took off with the owner of the massage school she was attending. She got her license and a new husband. Crazy, huh?"

I knew his parents had split up when he was in high school but not why. Rodrigo glanced over at me. "Not something I like to talk about."

"I'm so sorry. I thought your mother was married to a filmmaker?"

"That was husband number three. *Filmmaker* is overstating it. He made TV commercials and industrials… you know, corporate training videos. My mother left him after his big break never materialized and after he spent my college fund money on a bogus film project.

"You're kidding."

"My father left me some savings toward college, and her bonehead boyfriend convinced my mother to invest in his documentary that never happened. I honestly think that money went up his nose."

"How did you manage to get your degree, then?"

"I inherited some money from my grandmother, and I worked my ass off delivering pizzas."

Rodrigo was so humble about his tenacity and intelligence. I think I fell in love with him even more just then.

Chapter Eight

Rodrigo and I were standing above the Halona blowhole lookout point on the windward side of Oahu. As always, the churning, foamy, white tipped waves mesmerized me as a huge plume of ocean water erupted out of the blowhole. We were headed to Ginnie's memorial service after enjoying leisurely cups of Kona coffee and custard *malasadas* at our AirBnb rental. Rodrigo seemed a bit tentative as he stared out at the sparkling, clear, aquamarine ocean. He'd had a long conversation with his mother before breakfast, where he'd reluctantly agreed we'd meet her at her hotel for lunch. There had been lots of eyerolling and sighing as he paced back and forth with his phone on his shoulder and a mug of coffee. After he hung up, he sighed with resignation.

"Are there any malasadas left... or did we eat them all?"

"I think there are two left."

I went over to the kitchen table, opened the pink cardboard box of Leonard's malasadas, and handed Rodrigo one. He bit into the pillowy pastry and sighed with contentment.

"I can eat these every day."

"They're just like beignets."

"No, these are way better. I think I might be a malasada addict. Are there twelve step programs?"

I laughed as he walked over to the kitchen table and scarfed down the last one. He grabbed a paper towel at the kitchen sink and wiped his mouth, brushing away powdered white sugar.

"I guess it's time for you to officially meet my mother!" he said.

I laughed at his hangdog expression.

"She can't be that bad. She gave birth to you, after all."

"I can't explain my mother to you… you'll just have to see for yourself. I'm going to apologize now for her faults."

"It'll be fine."

That had been… *that*. Now a sadness crept into my chest as I thought about Ginnie's memorial service and my inevitable meeting with Jason. I wondered why I never openly grieved over the end of my twenty plus year marriage. There had been no tears… only an odd sense of finality. The only breakdown I'd had was when I found out my beloved yellow Labrador dog, *Ipo*, had died in his sleep post-divorce.

"You thinking about the memorial?" Rodrigo asked. He slipped his arm around my shoulders.

"No, I'm thinking of Ipo, my dog. He died right after my divorce was final. It was the worst day of my life. Ipo dying that is… not my divorce."

"You miss him."

"I honestly think I only hung onto the marriage because of Ipo. He was already twelve when I filed for divorce, and I left him with Jason because of his health problems. He had hip dysplasia and arthritis, and I knew I couldn't take him with me. He loved to sleep on the deck on his doggie bed overlooking the garden. The hardest day of my life was leaving him behind when I packed my things and left."

My eyes misted up as I recalled Ipo lying on his big, blue, denim dog bed, watching me avidly as I hauled my suitcases to the front door. He lifted his head briefly when I went over to pet him. His soulful brown eyes bore into mine as I explained why I was leaving.

"I'll give credit to Jason for nursing him up to the end. He cooked his food, gave him his vitamins and pain pills. In a weird way, Ipo's death symbolized the end of everything. He was the true beating heart of our lives together."

I brushed away tears as I thought of Ipo—the best dog ever.

Rodrigo took my hand and squeezed it. "You'll find another Ipo."

"No, I won't. But I might be open to getting another dog someday."

Rodrigo gave me a hug. "We should get going."

He took my hand and led me back to our compact rental car. We got in and buckled up. I realized as we got closer to Kailua, I didn't want to see Jason. I knew that if I suggested going to the North Shore instead, he'd turn the car around. However, I felt I owed it to Ginnie to show up to honor our unique friendship.

***

We stopped at the Starbucks in downtown Kailua. We were forty minutes early, so Rodrigo suggested we get some drinks.

"No more coffee for you," I insisted. "You've already had three cups."

He grinned. "Yes, ma'am… now I have to go pee!"

He moved toward the restrooms as I scanned the coffee menu. Then I saw *Lulu!* Her pink hair made her stand out from the crowd.

She turned as I shouted her name. What were the chances I'd run into my former landlady?

"My goodness… Noelani!"

We hurried toward each other and shared a fond embrace.

"What're you doing here?" I asked.

"My daughter signed us up for a weekend yoga workshop. Can you believe it… me doing yoga!" Lulu rolled her eyes and chuckled. She looked cute in a long-sleeved fuchsia top over matching sweatpants, hugging a large Coach tote bag with a cherry design to her side. Her outfit was completed with black Croc sandals.

"You look stylish in that outfit," I quipped.

Lulu sighed. "My daughter bought us matching Lululemon clothes. *So expensive… aieeee!*"

"I think that's sweet."

Lulu took my elbow and guided me away from the order line.

"Look at these prices for a cup of coffee. Criminal!"

She clucked her tongue and scanned the menu signboard with disapproval. Then a thought popped into my brain.

"Is someone named Braydon teaching the workshop?"

"I don't know. I have the flyer in my purse. She reached in and pulled out a folded flyer with Braydon's smiling visage on the front.

"That's the new yoga instructor at our lodge."

"Really? He better be good with the price he charges. Now, what are you doing here?"

I told her about the memorial service.

She glanced around, looking for Rodrigo. "Is your sexy man here too?"

I nodded toward the restrooms. "In the facilities. I'm glad he's with me, since Jason is here too."

"Are you going to be okay… I know Jason can mess you up sometimes."

I cringed inwardly. I regretted confiding about my miserable hook up with Jason with Lulu. *I'll never live THAT down!*

"I'm fine. I haven't seen him in over a year. I'm here for Ginnie… she was nice to me. In fact, Jason used to bemoan that Ginnie loved me more than him. Crazy, huh?"

"No, it's not crazy. You were the caring daughter she never had and her son was a selfish drunk."

I winced at Lulu's harsh words. I instinctively wanted to defend him but kept myself in check.

"Here's Rodrigo!" I chirped.

I was relieved to see him emerge from the restrooms, since I wanted to change the subject.

"Lulu—so nice to see you!" He leaned over and pecked her on the cheek.

Lulu blushed. "Oh I wish I were thirty years younger."

Rodrigo laughed. "You'll never age, Lulu."

"Let me buy you two some coffees. My daughter is running late… *as always*."

"We're fine." I said. "And Rodrigo has had too much caffeine today."

"Ice teas then. I insist!"

Before we could react, Lulu stepped into line to order. Rodrigo rubbed my back fondly. "Crazy running into her here, huh?"

"Lulu and her daughter are taking Braydon's yoga workshop. Isn't that wild?"

He shrugged. "It's a bit nuts."

"I'm glad we ran into her… it feels like a good omen."

He good-naturedly poked me in the ribs. *"You and your omens*!"

I ignored his jibe—I was too happy to see Lulu.

***

Kailua Beach was nearly empty except for a few kite surfers gliding on the water.

Rodrigo scanned the beach. "Where *is* everyone?" he asked.

"Dr. Serena is usually early for her bookings, so it's kind of weird."

We stared out at the limpid turquoise ocean. There was a gentle, balmy breeze that was refreshing. I'd donned a loose, tiered, red, pink, and blue floral cotton sundress with a straw hat. My skin already felt sticky. I dug into my straw beach tote and pulled out the memorial card. There was a grainy black and white photograph of Ginnie as a young nursing student and a recent color one. The card was elegantly engraved: "In loving memory of Virginia Johnson, Beloved mother of Jason and mother-in-law to Noelani Lee. Forever in our hearts." Inside the cream envelope was a white slip of paper with typed instructions to meet at Kailua Beach at one p.m. It also stipulated not to wear black. Rodrigo wore a nice, pale-blue Reyn Spooner dress shirt with a Monstera leaf pattern over khaki trousers and sandals.

"Well, we've got the right date and time. Not sure what's going on?" I said.

Rodrigo gestured at a group of people setting up a large, bright beach cabana. "Maybe that's them."

I craned my neck but couldn't make out what was going on.

"Come on," Rodrigo said. "Let's check it out."

He took my hand, and we slowly walked down a slope of warm, soft sand. As I got closer, I recognized Blake setting up some white, wooden folding chairs in a neat row. He looked especially handsome with his tanned face, tousled dirty blonde hair, and dark aviator sunglasses. He wore a light-blue Hawaiian print shirt over beige chino pants. He was barefoot.

"*Aloha!*" I called out.

"Aloha yourself," Blake said with a grin. He swept me up in a hug.

"Where is everyone?" I asked.

"You didn't get the text? Jason's plane got delayed yesterday and he just got in early this morning. So, we're not actually starting for another half hour or so. Plus, Dr. Serena got food poisoning and she couldn't even come. You look amazing, by the way!"

"You remember Rodrigo?"

Rodrigo stepped forward, and they shook hands. "You taking care of my girl?" Blake asked.

"Always."

"Well, let us help you set up," I said.

Rodrigo and I began to unfold chairs and put them aside as Blake lined them up.

"How many are coming?" I asked over my shoulder.

Blake shrugged. "Maybe twenty at most."

Rodrigo quickly unfolded ten chairs and turned toward me. "I'm going to run over to Whole Foods and get some bottled water."

"Okay."

As we watched him walk away, Blake made lip smacking noises.

"God, he is even more gorgeous than I remembered!"

"He's been working out more now that he's not working fulltime. How's Jason doing?"

"Okay I guess. You know he and Candace split up a while ago."

I felt relieved because I didn't want to run into her. "Really?"

"I knew it wouldn't last. The only thing that kept them together was the restaurant. They talked big about opening another one, but I don't think Jason was up to it. He's burned out."

Blake spoke over his shoulder as he methodically set up the remaining chairs in neat rows. After he'd arranged four rows with five chairs, he plopped down on a nearby chair with a sigh.

"He knows he blew it with you bigtime. He'll never admit it… being the narcissist that he is, but… *you snooze, you lose.*"

Blake's comments did little to comfort me. Even a few months ago, I would have reveled in hearing of Jason's suffering but now I just felt sad.

"Speaking of the devil, look who's here." Blake nodded toward the beach parking lot, and I saw my ex-husband walking toward us carrying a round, wooden urn topped with a pretty arrangement of bright-red ginger flowers, white orchid blossoms, and spikey orange protea stems. He was dressed in the Elvis Hawaiian shirt I'd last seen him wear, his eyes concealed behind reflective Oakley sunglasses. He'd lost weight, and his face was gaunt and drawn. My heart tightened at his emaciated appearance.

When he reached us, he shook Blake's hand and handed over the urn to him. Then he turned toward me. "Thanks for coming."

"Of course. Virginia was good to me."

"She loved you. You were the daughter she never had, so much so that she wanted you to have this."

He reached into his front pocket and pulled out a small, blue, velvet jewelry box and presented it to me. I opened it and saw Virginia's beautiful vintage diamond and sapphire cocktail ring.

"She always wore this," I said.

"She regretted not giving it to you in person."

"You should keep it. I know it was one of her favorites."

"No—it's for you."

I couldn't read Jason's expression. I remembered how he had a knack for being frustratingly enigmatic by hiding his feelings. I furrowed my brow irately and turned away from him, slipping the box into my purse.

"Where's your *fiancé?*" Jason smiled wanly as I turned back, facing the beach more than him.

"He'll be right back, he went to get some water."

"Good man."

Jason stuffed his hands into his khaki trousers, and an awkward silence fell between us.

"I heard your flight got delayed," I said finally.

He sighed. "Yeah. My luck's been pretty lousy lately. Dr. Serena couldn't come at the last minute."

"I heard."

To my surprise, he reached into his shirt pocket and took out a pack of cigarettes and a plastic lighter. He shook out a single cigarette and lit it, shooting me a mischievous smile as he exhaled a plume of cigarette smoke. I fanned the fumes away from my face.

"Do you mind?"

He chuckled. "Oh yeah, I forgot how you hated me smoking in front of you."

Asshole!

I wanted to retort but pursed my lips. I wasn't going to let him get under my skin.

"Hey, Jason… I could use some help setting up the altar," Blake called.

We both looked up to see Blake unfolding a wooden picnic table. Jason shrugged and walked toward him. I looked around for Rodrigo, but he hadn't returned yet, and I decided to walk down to the water. The pent up anxiety and dread I thought I'd feel hadn't materialized. I was surprised how detached I felt at seeing Jason— maybe I had finally moved on from all the hurt he had caused me? The powdery, alabaster sand felt good beneath my feet. I walked up to the water's edge and gazed out across the gently undulating turquoise waves. Suddenly, I saw a turtle head pop up about fifty yards in front of me. *Lono?* Just as I guessed it might be my shapeshifting friend, he paddled closer to shore.

"Yep…it's me!"

I nervously glanced around the shore. It was strictly illegal to interact with wildlife at the beaches, whether it was turtles or endangered monk seals. I could just imagine an official showing up and citing me an expensive fine. Lono intuited my misgivings.

"Hang on."

He ducked underneath a wave and re-emerged in his human form, only revealing himself from the waist up. I was so glad to see him, I almost ran into the water to hug him.

"Girlfriend!"

"I am so happy you're here."

"Kailani told me about the memorial service. I thought I'd lend some moral support. I sensed some distress."

"Attending a memorial service with my ex-husband present isn't my idea of fun," I confessed. "Plus, Rodrigo's been in a funk because his mother surprised him by popping up. And lastly... I feel so lame. Every time I want to tell Rodrigo about my mano self, I chicken out. I'm afraid he's going to freak out."

"Sounds like lots of drama."

I sighed. "Why can't life be simple?"

He chuckled. "Life *is* simple. It's just our human feelings and perspectives that muck everything up. Why did you come if you didn't want to?"

"I wanted to pay my final respects to Ginnie. She was always so kind to me. I felt like she cared for me much more than my own aunt, who raised me." My eyes welled up with tears as I recalled an especially poignant memory. "I had to have a laparoscopy once to see if I had an ovarian cyst, and she came out from Chicago. Jason was out-of-town on a business trip he couldn't cancel. Kailani wasn't available either, so Ginnie came. It was a day surgery—not a big deal."

"But she came anyway and acted like a real mother, right?"

I nodded and brushed away tears. She had ordered my favorite take-out food for dinner and even insisted on sitting with me until I fell asleep.

"You see... she was acting like a mother—something you've always hungered for. As for Rodrigo, he loves you completely, and sharing your mano self may be a shock, but he won't reject you because of it."

"You're right. I could never be authentic with Jason."

"I'm not criticizing your aunt. She taught you how important it was to fit in by always hiding your true feelings and not causing trouble. You had to earn her affection. I was that child also."

Hearing Lono say this caused my chest to tighten. Seeing Jason reminded me how fake my former life had been. I didn't allow myself to have needs or be genuinely heard or seen. His needs always came first, and that meant his over drinking that I put up with for so long.

"We're here for you, and we love you because of your true self."

I felt comforted by Lono's kind words. Before I could respond, I heard Rodrigo behind me. "Hey, Lono! What're you doing here?"

"Just chillin' with my favorite cuz."

"They're finally set up and ready to start the ceremony," Rodrigo said.

"I'll see you both back at the lodge," Lono said.

Rodrigo took my hand and we started back to the cabana. "You okay?" he asked.

"I was just sharing with Lono how special Ginnie was. I miss her."

Rodrigo slipped his arm around my shoulders. "I'm glad you had her in your life, Babe."

I couldn't stop the tears from flowing again.

Chapter Nine

The Outrigger Hotel was a popular and longtime presence in Waikiki and was always packed… today was no exception. Rodrigo and I sat in the comfortable, padded sofas inside the bustling hotel lobby. He looked handsome in a teal-green Reyn Spooner shirt with a faint bird of paradise print over khaki cargo shorts and black flip flops. He'd changed shirts three times. One shirt was too casual, another too formal, and I breathed a sigh of relief when he settled on the green shirt.

"You look great," I said.

He sighed and ran his hand over his newly cropped head and tapped his foot impatiently. The day before, we had stopped at a local barber, and he'd had his wavy locks chopped off for a modified buzz cut with some length on top and shaved on the sides. It made him look even sexier. I enjoyed the admiring looks from younger women as they passed by. Yep, this was *my man!*

"What's taking her so long?" he said.

"Why don't you call her?"

He sighed. "Maybe a buffet wasn't the best idea, seeing as she doesn't even eat meat."

"She eats seafood. They have garlic shrimp and a poke bowl option. Plus, they have a great salad bar here. Relax. She'll love it."

He flexed his fingers and checked his cell phone for the third time in five minutes. I should have been the nervous one, since I barely knew my future mother-in-law. A woman who was only ten years older than me. Yet I had enjoyed getting to know her over Zoom chats. She had a warm, welcoming presence, and I found myself confiding in her easily. She showed me sweet pictures of Rodrigo as a child, with interesting stories to match. It was obvious she loved him from the tender way she talked about him.

"By the way, your mother emailed a cute picture of you when you were like five at the zoo."

He looked up from his phone, his brows arched. "Really?"

"You don't remember? Margot said you asked why the animals were in jail. She said you looked so sad, it broke her heart."

He shook his head. "Don't remember that."

"Well, I doubt she'd make that up."

"I didn't say she lied, I said *I don't remember that.*"

I was taken aback by his sharp tone. "Someone woke up on the wrong side of the bed today."

"Sorry. I'm just feeling edgy. I hate it when she just shows up and pretends that everything is copacetic. She wasn't around for a chunk of my childhood. It felt like they were always fighting during my entire childhood. I was actually relieved when they finally split up for good when I was in high school. Then… it was just my dad and me."

"Have you tried talking to her… to clear the air?"

He shook his head. "I don't see the point. Let's just get through lunch, okay?"

I didn't respond. I knew when he was in a mood, it was better to retreat than to try to talk him off the ledge by saying comforting platitudes. Then I looked up and saw my future mother-in-law.

"There she is," I said.

Margot resembled the Northern California earth mama I'd envisioned when Rodrigo first showed me a photo of her on his Instagram account. That photo had been blurry but I could tell from all the colorful crystal jewelry she wore and her long, silvery hair she was your basic hippie crone. Today, Margot wore her hair in a thick braid over one shoulder. She had a long, wrinkled face with brown eyes and was dressed in a plum, crinkle cotton, sleeveless dress with flat, brown sandals. Several slim, silver bangle bracelets decorated both slender wrists. She also had on an elaborate silver moonstone pendant. She clutched an enormous straw tote bag to her side. We got up together as Margot embraced Rodrigo and kissed his cheek

"Aloha, Momma," Rodrigo said.

"You look good, son!"

She turned toward me and kissed both my cheeks fondly. "So nice to finally meet you, Noelani. I feel I already know you through our Zoom chats!"

"Thanks, Margot. You're much prettier in person."

"Aren't you sweet! Here, I brought you a little gift."

She reached into her tote bag and pulled out a small, cardboard, gold box with a pink ribbon.

"Go on, I'd like to see what you think." Margot said.

I untied the ribbon easily and took off the box lid. Inside was a black heart pendant on a silver chain. The stone was set in a delicate filigree base.

"Thank you, Margot, it's lovely."

I unclasped the necklace but struggled with the tiny, delicate clasp. Margot reached over and clasped it for me.

"It looks nice on you," Rodrigo said.

"It's made of obsidian—perfect for grounding your energy."

Rodrigo sighed loudly. "I'm going to use the restroom and check on our table."

We watched him stride away.

"I think I've upset him. He hates it when I talk about airy fairy stuff." Margot lifted her shoulders and smiled with resignation. "He's like his father—not much for the mystical aspects of life, I'm afraid."

"I think he's opening up. We have friends who talk about nature spirits like the *menehunes* and it doesn't bother him. He thinks it's funny."

"*Menehunes?*"

"They're kind of like elves."

"Elves! How fun is that? How are you doing? How was the memorial service?"

"It was fine. Rodrigo was a huge support."

Before I could respond, a pert, young hostess appeared with menus. Rodrigo walked up just in time.

"Rodrigo… party of three?"

"That's us," he said.

She gestured for us to follow her, and we ventured into the cavernous, open air dining room with an expansive view of the large, limpid, teal-blue hotel pool We were seated near the opulent buffet sideboard, and the tantalizing smell of Kahlua pork and Teriyaki chicken wafted invitingly. Our server, a young Asian man, greeted us with a warm smile just as a busser appeared with glasses of ice water.

"Aloha folks, are we doing the buffet today?"

Rodrigo nodded, "The best buffet in town!"

Margot watched intently as the busser placed the glasses on the table. "Is the water filtered?" she asked.

"I can assure you the tap water is safe to drink."

"Mom, water on Oahu is some of the cleanest," Rodrigo replied.

Margot stared at the water glasses suspiciously. "I'm sure you're right."

"Shall we check out the buffet?" I interjected.

We all got up, with Rodrigo gently cupping my elbow as he steered me toward the poke bowl counter.

"Oh my God… she never stops," he sighed.

We glanced behind us and saw Margot standing at the salad bar, questioning the attendant.

"I know she's asking if the produce is organic or not. We should have gone somewhere else." His lips tightened with irritation.

"She should have met us at the lodge. Shara and she would hit it off with the *no plastic* rule and the fact that they grow everything organically," I quipped.

"Let's try to get through this," Rodrigo said.

I watched with amusement as Margot filled her dinner plate with salad greens. Rodrigo did the opposite and filled his plate with Kalbi beef ribs, garlic shrimp, and Teriyaki chicken. I started with a tuna poke bowl. We all made it back to the table and sat down. The raw tuna chunks were delicately seasoned with soy sauce and was refreshing for a hot day. Margot seemed to enjoy her salad without comment, while Rodrigo wolfed down his meat with happy grunting sounds.

"You know, when Rodrigo was a child, he used to separate his food. He'd push the peas to one side, then the potatoes and the chicken. He hated everything touching… it'd upset him."

"Mom… you're exaggerating a little, aren't you?"

"I finally had to get stainless steel plates with partitions to make him happy. They looked like something used in a prison, but they were easy to clean."

Rodrigo sighed. "We got them because Dad would get upset and break the ceramic plates. That was the real reason."

Margot stared intently at her salad. "He was clumsy."

I didn't comment and focused on my poke bowl. I heard a squawking sound and looked up to see a large black crow land at an empty table near us. The bird tilted its head to one side and cawed loudly. *Kailani?*

"Hi, girlfriend… having fun yet?" Kailani's cheerful voice popped into my head.

"I feel like a referee. I think Margot's nice, but… family drama!"

"It happens."

Kailani flapped her wings and Margot looked up.

"What a beautiful bird. Crows are an auspicious sign."

"Awwww thank you. Your mother-in-law has great taste!"

"Crows represent transformation and magic," she added.

Rodrigo made no comment as he wolfed down his food.

"That's interesting," I said.

"Right before Rodrigo's father and I split up, a crow landed on the windshield of my car. I knew it was a sign that we would divorce."

"What happened to that Mazda Miata?" Rodrigo asked.

"I sold it to buy a used RV and hit the road. Total freedom!"

Rodrigo got up. "Time for seconds."

A server came by and waved at Kailani. "Go on… *get out!*"

"How rude," Kailani said and flew off.

Margot leaned closer to me and put her hand over mine. "I'm sorry if my son is a bit out-of-sorts. We seem to constantly trigger each other. I know he hasn't forgiven me for his crazy childhood. I tried my best," Margot said.

"He said you were pretty young when you had him."

She nodded and gazed out at the hotel pool. "I was a foolish young woman. I craved attention and approval. When it came to picking partners, I had poor judgment."

"It happens to the best of us."

"I was swept away by Rodrigo's father. He was thirty-five, and he seemed so worldly. He had beautiful, long, wavy, chestnut-brown hair and the kindest eyes. A lovely hazel green." Margot sighed. "I got pregnant right away, and he felt duty bound to marry me. My mother wanted me to put the baby up for adoption. She knew of a convent that would have taken me in. But I couldn't bear the thought of my baby being given away to strangers. I wasn't the perfect mother, I know that."

Poor Rodrigo. It must have been so tough weathering a chaotic childhood. Aunt Lily hadn't been perfect, but she had been a steady presence in my life. My heart contracted sympathetically thinking about how wonderfully he turned out. He was so caring and kind.

Rodrigo bounded back to the table with a grin and waved his iPhone at me.

"I got a booking for tomorrow. A couple staying at The Prince… you don't mind staying an extra night, do you? They booked a ninety minute session… *each*."

"Sounds good… how'd you get the booking?"

"Some friends of Shara and Kailani… I'm so stoked."

Margot clapped her hands together. "That's awesome. Noelani and I can spend more time together."

Before I could react, I heard Kailani's gleeful voice in my head: *"Good times, girlfriend. Your mother-in-law is a hoot!"*

"I didn't realize crows had such a droll sense of humor?" I replied.

"All highly evolved beings have a great sense of humor… just like me!"

I didn't know how to respond to *that*.

As Rodrigo chowed down on his second helping of Kalbi beef, Margot frowned. He looked up. "What, Mom?"

"Do you always eat so much meat? It's not good to consume so much red meat. I worried about your father eating so many barbequed steaks."

Rodrigo sighed impatiently. "Mom, we're all going to die from something."

"We don't eat that much meat," I quickly added. "They serve only vegetarian food at the lodge."

"That's wonderful."

An awkward silence fell, and I got up to load more salad on my plate, Rodrigo springing up beside me. As we moved toward the buffet, Rodrigo leaned closer to me.

"Sorry my mother's such a pain-in-the-ass."

"She's just worried about your health. She told me your paternal grandfather died from colon cancer. So there is *that.*"

"He did? That's news to me."

"She told me a lot of things about your family."

"Like what?"

I shrugged. "Like how loving and warm your dad's family was. How they accepted her with open arms, especially your dad's mother, Camila, who taught her how to cook Portuguese food."

"I don't remember Mom ever cooking us Portuguese food."

I didn't want to challenge his memories or *lack thereof.* So I shifted the subject to his favorite topic… *food.*

"The garlic shrimp is extra tasty today."

"I'm going to get some more of that."

I watched him move off toward the hot buffet bar as I made my way back to the table. Margot was picking at her salad.

"I guess we should have picked a different restaurant that was more to your liking," I said apologetically.

"This is fine. The view is lovely, and it's close to my hotel. The salad bar is fresh."

Rodrigo returned and sat down. He'd loaded up with more beef and shrimp and happily dug into them.

"I told Rodrigo how you liked to cook Portuguese food you learned from your ex-mother-in-law."

Margot beamed. "Yes, Camila was a fabulous cook. She made this amazing seafood rice."

"Kind of like cioppino?" I asked.

Margot shook her head. "No… it's hard to describe."

"She made this bread soaked in broth, too," Rodrigo said.

"*I remember that!*" Margot said.

"She always cooked for dad and me. She made an amazing duck rice, too."

"Yes she did."

"I'm glad you have fond memories of your grandmother," I said.

He smiled, glanced at Margot, and nodded tacitly.

Chapter Ten

Kuhio Beach Park was my favorite Waikiki beach. It felt intimate and safe thanks to the high retaining wall that encircled it. I could easily relax into the gentle, warm waves and float. I suggested Margot meet me there since she was staying nearby and could easily walk over. I got there early to swim and scanned the beach. I took in the gentle turquoise water and fine, opalescent sand as I threw down my beach towel. I kicked off my sandals, peeled off my cotton cover up, and walked over to the water's edge, wading in slowly and enjoying the warm water lapping over my bare feet and calves. I plunged in and kicked my way through the waves. A euphoric sense of freedom enveloped me as I used my arms to breaststroke deep into the ocean. I loved being fully submerged and bobbing along with the currents. I enjoyed the silence. It was also so freeing not to wear a bulky snorkeling face mask. I was safe and unencumbered as I fluidly whooshed through the salty water. A tingling sensation started on the sides of my neck as my gills opened and flexed. An electrical current rippled through my body as a school of colorful parrotfish swam lazily past me. I spotted teal, purple, and coral fish as they passed me unhurriedly. Another school of zebra striped tang fish soon followed. They reminded me of my own goldfish that I'd kept in my round fish tank in my bedroom.

After a while, I kicked my way up to the surface. Shafts of brilliant sunlight illuminated my journey back up, and I was bathed with incandescent light. As I got closer to shore, I stood up awkwardly and nearly fell over. It was still a tough transition from mano mode to back being on land. My legs felt leaden as I trudged awkwardly on the sand.

I self-consciously patted the side of my neck, but the gills had disappeared. I found my bright-blue, floral beach towel and plopped down, forking my fingers through my wet hair as I took a breath. Breathing normally felt strange, but I forced myself to take even gulps of air. After sluicing through the ocean effortlessly, it was a chore to actually breathe. I looked up and noticed a woman and her daughter set up nearby. The little girl looked to be about four or five, with a cute Disney *Moana* themed swimsuit. The top had an orange bow with the pig, and the bottom was a ruffled swim skirt. She had a mop of wavy hair and a cute, round, chubby face.

"Very cute!" I said.

The mother looked up with a smile. She was probably late twenties, with a big, floppy, straw hat and a complementary orange crop top and sarong that matched the little girl's outfit.

"She loves *Moana*… we've seen the movie fifty times!" she joked. Then to her daughter, "Violet, say thank you."

She looked up with a shy smile. "Thank you."

I watched as Violet's mother spread out their beach blanket and fished out a bottle of sunscreen from her tote bag.

"Come here, honey."

Violet obediently sat down cross legged as her mother squirted sunscreen on her back and arms. She tenderly smoothed the lotion on Violet's skin. A bittersweet feeling bubbled up inside me as I watched them interact. I wished I'd had an affectionate mother who fussed over me. At the same time, Violet's innocence and sweetness charmed me.

"There you are!"

I looked up to see Margot standing over me, wearing a long, pale-blue chambray shirtdress with a wide brimmed, straw sun visor. A huge straw bag was slung over her shoulder. Oval, white, retro sunglasses completed her outfit, and I found myself staring at miniature twin reflections of myself.

"You found me," I said.

"Do you mind if we move somewhere with shade?"

"Sure."

I gathered my things and waved at Violet, who was happily shoveling sand into a plastic pail. Her mother had put up an umbrella and was reading, lounging on a beach chair.

"I'm sorry to be a bother," Margot said.

"It's fine. This heat takes getting used to."

"I'm a mountain person. I love the cool and damp and being surrounded by trees. I lived for a while in Mendocino."

"In your RV?"

Margot looked puzzled. "No, in a cabin."

"Yesterday you mentioned you sold your car to buy an RV, so I thought…"

"I never had an RV."

I raised my eyebrows in confusion. *But she did say she owned an RV!* Something strange happened. The sides of my neck began to tingle. I immediately touched my neck but didn't feel the gills. *Thank God!*

"Sorry, I guess I misunderstood," I blurted.

I distinctly remembered her comment previously about selling the Mazda. I wasn't sure what was going on.

We found a small, shaded spot beneath a palm tree, and Margot fished out a striped beach towel with a hotel logo and flopped down with a sigh. She also pulled out a big bottle of coconut water and took a generous swig.

"So important to stay hydrated." She sighed.

I laid out my own beach towel alongside hers, and she handed me an unopened bottle of organic coconut water.

"I've got my water bottle," I said.

"You've got to keep hydrated with electrolytes… plain water isn't enough."

I accepted the coconut water with a grateful smile.

"Do you have a close friend with a 'G' name? Like Gina or Georgia?" Margot asked abruptly. I furrowed my brows in confusion.

"No… why do you ask?"

"I'm getting a message for you from someone with a 'G' name."

My mind filtered through my friend's names: *Kailani, Cassie, Diana… Lulu?* I shook my head. Margot's eyes had a faraway, dreamy look. She tilted her head to one side and went silent.

"It's a relative, I think."

I shook my head again. *What is going on?*

"It's an older woman. I'm getting a name… *Ginnie!*"

"My mother-in-law." My mouth fell open. *Okay, this is getting surreal.* Margot saw my wide eyes and open mouth and laughed. "Ginnie wanted to leave you more jewelry. There was a diamond ring. A platinum band with three rows of diamonds. Hmmmm." Margot scrunched her face up in concentration. "Your ex-husband gave it to a blonde haired woman. Ginnie said she forgot to include that diamond ring in her will, and she's upset you didn't get it." Margot let out a sigh. "Your former husband was a piece of work."

"It's a long story."

"Ginnie said to look at your social media account for proof."

"My social media account?" I echoed.

I reached for my phone and pulled up my Instagram account. I saw an old post from Jason and wondered why I hadn't deleted him earlier. He had posted pictures of himself with Candace. She was holding up keys, and the caption read, "A new chapter. Follow us on X for announcements about our new business venture!" I zoomed in on her hand holding the keys. There was Ginnie's diamond ring on the ring finger of her right hand. Margot looked over at me with concern.

"What's wrong?"

I held up my phone and showed her Candace's photo. *"Oh dear."*

I was surprised that I wasn't more upset. I folded my arms across my chest and shook my head. I found myself cringing. "What a jerk. I can't believe I was so clueless this whole time."

Margot put her hand on my shoulder. "At least he's in the rearview mirror. Good for you that you left. This woman gives him purpose, and she has vision. I'm assuming they're starting another restaurant venture together."

"They *were.* She's history now."

"I know he truly loved you and that frightened him. But he isn't a man who can give you his whole heart. Maybe it seemed that way in the beginning, but you deserve much more."

I never thought of myself as a violent person, but at that moment, I wished a rogue wave had knocked Jason down at the memorial and swept him out to sea. I took grim satisfaction at the thought of him thrashing helplessly as he got swallowed up by the ocean.

"I am so gullible. I felt sorry for him at the memorial service. Ugh!"

"You are very tender hearted. That's why Rodrigo fell in love with you. When he met you, he texted me and told me he found his soulmate. I was in shock… he never said that about any of his past girlfriends. There weren't many, but I worried he'd end up alone. Not that he confided much in me. When he texted your picture, I knew immediately you were The One."

"I didn't know that. He called me his *soulmate*?" My chest squeezed with happiness.

"I've never seen him so happy," Margot affirmed.

I looked into Margot's face and saw the genuine love for her son in her glowing smile.

"Please don't let your ex-husband take up real estate in your mind."

"Rodrigo never mentioned you had psychic abilities."

Margot laughed. "He doesn't believe in all this *airy fairy* stuff—I'm sure you're quite aware of that!" Her eyes crinkled with amusement. "I'm an elemental earth witch. I bond with nature spirits and the earth mother. I also receive information through *clairalience* which is a pain sometimes."

"*Clairalience?*"

Margot pointed to her nose with a grin. "My bullshit meter is a strong sense of smell. Right now, I smell something flowery, and I see a blue container with white doves on the lid."

My scalp prickled. "That's body powder my Aunt Lily used to wear called Rapture." A brief memory of my aunt sitting on her bed, powdering herself with a big powder puff while wearing her pink terrycloth robe floated to mind.

"She's standing next to you and smiling. She's gesturing at me," Margot narrowed her eyes in concentration. "She said she's glad you got the money back from your ex-husband."

The sides of my neck pulsed, and a strange wooziness rippled through me. I took a deep breath to settle myself. My gills seemed to be acting as a truth barometer.

"She likes the ring that your ex-husband's mother left you. Now I'm seeing a yellow perfume box. The perfume bottle has a fancy top with two birds."

"My aunt used to wear L'air du Temp perfume."

Margot nodded. "She had such a hard life. She never married."

I nodded. "She didn't show any interest in men at all."

"She had a special friend named Eva? They spent time together in college."

Eva? I vaguely remembered seeing postmarked envelopes with the return address as Eva… *something.*

Margot shut her eyes briefly. "They were very close."

"You mean like… more than friends?" The epiphany surprised me. I remembered asking Aunt Lily about the letters and why they stopped coming. She just shook her head with a sad smile.

Margot opened her eyes and shook her head. "I don't know. Sometimes I'm not allowed to see more."

"Wow. She might have had a girlfriend." The revelation startled me. Aunt Lily rarely confided in me or even talked about herself. She had always been a mystery to me.

"Being gay back then wasn't discussed," Margot said gently. She reached over and patted my hand. "I'm so happy you and Rodrigo met. You're starting a new chapter together—a glorious one."

I smiled at her kind words. Inside, my emotions were roiling. *My future mother-in-law is a witch!*

Chapter Eleven

Rodrigo looked especially handsome in a white polo shirt with the lodge logo over his swim trunks. We laid our beach towels on the damp grass and sat down. The pristine, aquamarine waters rippled gently beneath the sunny sky. The briny smell of saltwater filled my nose. He kicked off his flip flops and squatted down, stretching his legs out with a contented sigh.

"This is the life!" he sighed.

A ripple of happiness fanned through me. I liked seeing his wide smile and relaxed face. It was a quintessential beach day, starting with the boundless turquoise sky and the cotton-like puffs of pearly clouds. We'd found a partially shaded spot on the grass overlooking Carlsmith Beach. I put down a straw tote bag that contained our lunch—grilled veggie sandwiches wrapped in wax paper from the lodge kitchen. I'd also put two stainless steel bottles of water and paper napkins inside the tote.

He leaned over and rubbed my back affectionately. "How're you doing, sweetie? You seem a little out-of-sorts," he asked.

"I'm okay. I just had a weird dream last night."

"Tell me."

I hesitated. Part of me wanted to just forget about it, but part of me was haunted by the grim images. It was a recurring dream about being stuck in an elevator. My Aunt Lily is inside the elevator, she beckons me to come closer. She looks scared and grabs my hand. She squeezes my hand so tightly, it hurts. *"It's happening again!"* she shouts. Suddenly, the elevator plummets down at a terrifying velocity. I gripped the handrails, hoping to brace myself, and screamed loudly for help. I knew that it wasn't long before I'd crash into the lobby and die. Then I heard Dr. Serena yelling at me to lie down on the floor. *"You'll survive if you lie down—have faith."* At the last moment, the elevator screeched to an abrupt halt.

I described the nightmare to him and shuddered.

"That sounds horrible. What do you think it means?"

"I'm not sure."

"Fear of losing control?"

I shrugged. "I used to have falling dreams when I was little. Like… plummeting through space, and I'd land on my bed and wake up."

Rodrigo reached into the tote bag and pulled out one of the water bottles. He took a swig and offered me a drink. I shook my head.

"Those childhood nightmares left me feeling hopeless and terrified. My aunt used to scold me for wetting the bed when I had the dreams."

Rodrigo reached over and put his hand over mine. "Your aunt was a piece of work, man."

"She's been dead for a while, and yet she still pops up in my dreams."

Rodrigo shook his head. "As a kid, I had nightmares like that. Now I rarely even remember my dreams."

"Maybe the dream is showing me something I haven't resolved from the past."

"My mother keeps telling me that everything is a work in progress. She's done psychotherapy, hypnosis, and who knows what. She even went to a shaman in the rain forest and did an ayahuasca ceremony. I'm not sure how any of it was helpful."

"That's *a lot.*"

Rodrigo took another swig of water. "Before I forget, Braydon and Lono invited me to bike down Haleakalā with them." Rodrigo paused as he watched my reaction. I tilted my head to one side. *Is he asking for my permission?*

"The three of you are going to bike down Haleakalā?"

He dipped his head down. "I'd like your blessing."

"Of course you can go." My stomach tightened at the thought of him flying down the side of the volcano. Horrific images flooded my mind of him flying over the handlebars and crashing, headfirst. My stomach clenched up at the nerve-wracking scenario.

"I want us to be able to support each other in pursuing our dreams," I said.

He exhaled sharply, then reached over and rubbed my back fondly. "I'm glad you're okay with it."

Of course I'm not okay with it! People seemed to die accidentally all the time in Hawaii… although it was mainly by drowning. I'd read that there was at least one drowning every week. Surprisingly, fatalities on Haleakalā were rare, despite the rugged, twisting terrain. Still… cyclists had actually died. My chest tightened.

"You really didn't say how things went with my mother."

"It was fine—we had a nice time hanging out."

I guiltily thought of the money in the envelope that I'd hidden away at the bottom of dresser drawer.

"She gifted us some money to put toward the wedding."

"Oh yeah… like a couple hundred dollars?"

"A bit more than that."

"A thousand dollars?"

"Five thousand dollars."

Rodrigo's eyes widened. "Where'd she get that kind of money?"

"I didn't ask her, and she didn't volunteer that information."

Rodrigo jutted his chin out. "We can't accept it."

"Why not?"

What is going on with him? Why is he being so stubborn?

"I feel like she's trying to buy her way into our affections or something. Like she's trying to make up for my college money fiasco."

"Well, what's wrong with that?"

"You wouldn't understand." Rodrigo's face clouded over and he fell silent.

"I think it's a nice gesture."

He sighed. "I can see you want to keep it."

I put my hands up in surrender. "I don't want to fight about this. I have no problem returning the money."

"If you're worried about money, *don't*. I was going to bring it up sooner, but I have a Zoom meeting with a job recruiter scheduled next week."

It was my turn to be surprised. "I thought you said you were casually looking? This sounds serious."

"I'm not committed to anything except talking to him about running a physical therapy clinic in Arizona."

"*Arizona?*"

"We're just going to talk, but it's crazy good money." His face brightened. "It'd be a great opportunity—we could afford to buy a house there."

Arizona? What is he thinking? I'd spent a week accompanying Jason on a business trip there. It was hotter than hell.

"I thought we were going to make this our home?"

"We've stuck it out for almost a year. I'm glad we tried it, but I'm making half of what I was back in California. I'm looking out for *us* and our future—putting down roots by buying a home together."

"In *Arizona.*"

He grimaced at my lack of enthusiasm.

"We could fly back and forth," Rodrigo said. "Don't you want to have a house again and settle down?"

"I just feel we're rushing into things. It's only been a year, and I'm happy here."

"I get that. You just said we want to be able to support each other's dreams. Buying a home and putting down roots is something I thought you wanted."

"It is. Can we table this for after the wedding?"

"Sure. Is there anything else you want to talk about?"

"Like?"

He leaned over and brushed the side of my neck with his index finger. "I've been meaning to ask about *this.*"

So… here's an opening. I could tell him about my mano self. My heart started drumming hard and my face went hot.

"What do you mean?"

Rodrigo leaned over and inspected my neck. "I don't see it now, but sometimes it looks like some kind of birthmark? Do you cover it with makeup?"

I touched my neck self-consciously. I noticed lately that the gills seemed to recede slower, and I worried they wouldn't go away at all.

"It's kind of like a birthmark. It's genetic."

"You don't have to cover it up. I think you're perfect." Rodrigo smiled tenderly. "Just be who you are."

"What if I'm like part fish or something?"

He laughed. "Now you're starting to sound like my crazy mother. What do you mean part fish?"

"I mean…" I swallowed hard and my mouth went dry. "I just found this out… I'm part shark."

Rodrigo's face went blank. I could see the wheels turning, and my stomach clenched up.

"You're joking, right?"

I jumped up. "I'll show you, then."

I hurried over to the water's edge and waded in. I knelt down to submerge my face and neck, then stood back up, my hair loose and dripping wet around my shoulders. I felt the gills sprouting out and walked back to Rodrigo, turning my head. An intense swirl of emotions threatened to overwhelm me. Vulnerability, anxiety, and fear stabbed at me.

"I wanted to tell you a long time ago."

His eyes widened with shock. *What the hell?*

My face reddened. "I know it's a lot to take in," I said haltingly.

"I've been having sex with a… *fish*?"

Rodrigo's comical outburst made me laugh nervously. "Kind of… *yes.*"

"*Holy shit.* So… are you a shapeshifter or something?"

I nodded. "I wanted to tell you," I repeated. "I was just afraid of how you'd react. Are you okay?"

Rodrigo jumped to his feet. "I guess so… I don't know. I mean, you've been keeping this secret from me, and it's a huge secret." He paced back and forth on the grass, wringing his hands. "I mean… why would you keep this from me? What else are you holding back on? I mean… *fuck!*"

"That's all. I swear!"

Rodrigo sucked in a slow breath. "I don't know what to think. I'm seriously weirded out right now."

Tendrils of fear rose up in me. My skin got clammy. My worst fears suddenly materialized as I witnessed Rodrigo's horrified reaction.

"It's still *me.* I'm still the same person." I quavered unconvincingly. I was trying not to lose it, but my heart was pounding so hard, my rib cage ached.

"Are you, though? What if you completely transform into a shark… then what?"

"I don't think that'll happen. I have some control of that."

"Do you?" Rodrigo's face hardened and his eyes narrowed.

Hot tears formed at the corners of my eyes. I brushed them away impatiently with the back of my hand. "*This* was what I was afraid of. That you'd freak out and—"

"*What the fuck*? You've kept this big secret this whole time and I'm supposed to just go… it's okay, babe. *We're good. Fuck!*"

"I was scared!" I bleated helplessly.

Rodrigo tossed his head. "We're going back to the lodge." He briskly gathered up our things, while I stood frozen, a sickening feeling of hopelessness washing over me. My arms hung uselessly at my sides. He stomped off toward the lodge van, and I followed slowly behind him. He refused to look at me on the drive back.

When we pulled up in front of the kitchen, he got out hurriedly and slammed the van door loudly, stomping toward the cabin, then stopped and turned. I cowered at his withering glare.

"Give that money back. I'm not sure about the wedding."

I burst into loud tears at his harsh words, covering my eyes with my hands, my shoulders heaving uncontrollably as I broke down sobbing.

"Hey." I looked up and saw Kailani at the open van window. She reached over and put a comforting hand on my shoulder. It just made me cry harder.

"He's left me," I moaned. Kailani opened the van door and helped me out. Shara was behind her. As I leaned unsteadily against my best friend, she draped her arm around my shoulders and drew me in for a consoling squeeze. Then they both embraced me in a tight hug. That lifelong fear that had haunted me all my life had come true once again. Someone I loved deeply had rejected me, because I didn't deserve to be loved.

Chapter Twelve

Kailani poured me a glass of plantation iced tea and pushed a plate of Shara's mango muffins toward me across the wooden buffet table.

"Remember when I found out Declan cheated on me with Trixie James?" I said.

Kailani sighed. "I know—he was a total shit."

I remembered the intense misery I felt after finding out my high school boyfriend had slept with a popular cheerleader. Trixie James was perfect, with luminous, poreless skin, thick, fringed eyelashes and long, toned legs. She had turned heads all the time. Now those abject feelings of insecurity rose up and consumed me. I was that sixteen-year-old teenager filled with hopelessness that I'd been abandoned by someone I trusted. *I screwed up…it's all my fault that Rodrigo is so upset with me. Why didn't I just tell him upfront and trust him?*

"It's not the same situation. Declan was pathetic and immature. This is just a *misunderstanding.*" Kailani leaned over and patted my hand.

"It's a lot for him to process. Give him time—they've only been gone three days," she added.

Three days ago! It seemed a lot longer that Lono, Braydon, and Rodrigo had driven off in Lono's truck. I'd stood on the patio of the lodge kitchen, watching them excitedly load their bikes into the truck. Rodrigo didn't even look my way as he climbed into the truck cab. Braydon scrambled into the flatbed and waved cheerfully as they rumbled down the driveway. I hadn't heard from Rodrigo at all. Then I received a text from Lono saying they decided to stay an extra day, and my stomach constricted. *What is going on?* I missed Rodrigo the most when I turned over at night to the empty space next to me in bed.

"Do you remember how I found out about Declan cheating on me?

Kailani shook her head.

"It was right after graduation. We always had our Saturday night date at Pizza Heaven and then went to the movies. I hadn't heard from him in a few days, so I called his house. His mother answered. She was a night nurse, and when I called, I woke her up. She just said he was out with someone named Trixie and hung up."

"Oh my God—you're right. You called me, and I borrowed my grandmother's car and we drove to Pizza Heaven."

"And there he was, with Trixie," I said with a resigned sigh. *First Declan... then Jason. Am I just a magnet for cheating partners? The two men I trusted the most.*

"Did I tell you Declan called me and begged me to talk to you? Basically, he wanted me to convince you to give him a second chance," Kailani said.

"He *did?*"

She nodded. "Rumors were that Trixie dumped him because she was only with Declan to make her boyfriend jealous. He was desperate. He told me he never did the deed with Trixie. He said they only made out a few times. I told him to fuck off—*you snooze, you lose!*" Kailani grinned mischievously. Her words should have amused me. In present time, I felt regret that I had totally ghosted him and didn't bother to give him a chance to explain himself. I threw away his letters, I hung up on him when he tried to call, and I stared straight ahead when he tried to talk to me. Even at our twentieth high school reunion, I'd pretended not to see him. Now I wondered if Rodrigo would give me a chance to explain myself. My stomach knotted with worry.

"Why do you think they're staying an extra day? Did you hear anything else from Lono?"

Is Rodrigo staying away longer to avoid confronting me? Is he contemplating breaking up with me? Is he going to pack up his things and go back to California without me? The disquieting worries mingled with a scary dream I'd had the previous night of Rodrigo falling off his bike and bashing his head on a rock. In true cartoon fashion, his head exploded with blood and his eyes rolled up until he blacked out. I'd awakened soaked in sweat with my heart pounding so hard, I thought it would pop out of my chest.

Kailani shrugged. "He just said they were having lots of fun and decided to stay a little longer. I wouldn't stress out over it."

I didn't tell Kailani I'd made an emergency phone call to Dr. Serena. Unfortunately, she was doing a womens retreat on Mt. Shasta and wouldn't be back for a week. I felt stuck in an endless feedback loop of childhood angst. *People leave me, I'm doomed to be alone!* Intellectually, I knew this wasn't true, but the fear kept its ironclad grasp on me. I watched Kailani and Shara lovingly interact every day and wondered why Kailani didn't have the same phobia I did? We had similar childhoods of being raised by relatives instead of loving parents—yet she always seemed well-adjusted and happy.

"You're coming to the full moon meditation tonight, right?" Kailani asked.

I shook my head. "I'd rather be alone."

"Tonight is a strawberry full moon, which represents the heart. It'd be good for you to come. Just come in late and sit in the back near the door. Then you can leave quickly when the ceremony is over."

The kitchen door banged open, and Shara emerged carrying a wicker basket of freshly picked herbs. The savory scent of fresh basil wafted pleasantly into the kitchen. Shara set the basket down on the granite counter and tenderly cupped Kailani's face in her hands. "Hey, beautiful."

They exchanged a sweet, lingering kiss, and Shara pulled Kailani in for a warm embrace. My face reddened with embarrassment. It was such a natural and intimate moment, I felt like I was intruding. "Amazing." Kailani sighed as she leaned over and sniffed the basket.

"Time to make my world-famous pesto grilled veggies for dinner tonight!" Shara said.

I felt a pang of envy as I watched them interact. They seemed so settled and content. *I used to have that with Jason.* I wondered if I'd ever have it with Rodrigo. Would he get tired of me in a few years when I turned sixty and he would only be forty four? What if he changed his mind and decided he wanted children? Sometimes I saw younger women and imagined how happier he would be with a fitter, fecund woman. What if he wanted someone who could keep up with him on his brisk, daily runs? Or loved to go on strenuous hikes? *That isn't me.*

I got up and drank down the last of my tea and took the mug to the sink. It slipped out of my hand and shattered when it landed in the sink.

"Oh God. I'm sorry!" I gasped.

Kailani gently waved me off. "I got this. Why don't you go for a walk to clear your mind?"

"Go down to Lookout Point. I always find it restful to just stare at the ocean," Shara suggested.

I slipped out the front door. The last thing I saw was Shara and Kailani hugging affectionately without a care in the world.

I headed down the muddy single track path toward the driveway. Lookout Point was located at the end of the paved driveway across the road. It was a rocky outcropping overlooking the ocean. There was a wooden bench nestled at the tip of the cliff, looking straight down at the jagged rocks below.

I kept thinking of how easy life had turned out for Kailani, and a bubble of resentment percolated inside me. From the moment they met in college, they had shared a strong connection. Even after Shara surprised Kailani when she impulsively eloped with her college boyfriend, they'd maintained a steady friendship. They never seemed to bicker, or if they did, Kailani never mentioned it. After Shara's divorce, when she wanted to attend nursing school at UT Austin, Kailani had cheerfully packed up and went with her to Texas. They'd flourished in the Keep Austin Weird vibe and even found an amazing vegan restaurant near their modest apartment. I knew I wouldn't be happy in the suffocating heat of Arizona, but I wanted to be with Rodrigo.

I was barely five minutes away from Lookout Point when my phone rang. It was Cassie. *Great… of course Miss Perfect Life would call me now!* My stomach clenched—I thought about letting the call roll into voicemail, but a jab of guilt compelled me to answer even though she was the last person I wanted to talk to.

"Hey, girlfriend!" Cassie said.

"Hey yourself."

"How're things in paradise?"

"Okay. How're things with you?"

"You sound stressed. What's going on?

My lips pressed together tightly.

"Nothing."

A stab of irritation started in my stomach, and my jaw tightened. I heard traffic noise in the background and Cassie's sighing impatiently.

"I'm in the middle of godawful traffic on my way to pick up the kiddo from swim camp."

I could feel the tension in Cassie's tone. I dreaded the thought of going back to the urban craziness of California if Rodrigo and I returned to the states. Avoiding the relentless busyness of city life was why we moved to the islands. Then my chest squeezed anxiously. *If we're still together, that is.* I wasn't in the mood to listen to Cassie's over dramatic complaints of her first world problems. I changed the subject to something more agreeable.

"How're things with hubby and the bambino?"

"Don't get me started. *Hey, asshole, turn on your fucking turn signal!* Sorry, some dickwad just cut me off. I wish I was there with you guys. What was I thinking having a baby at this age? I think I'm in full blown menopause. I haven't had a period in like three months, and I feel like *shit.*"

I sighed loudly and looked up at the sky. *How could I give up clear, cornflower blue skies for congested rush hour traffic?*

"This too shall pass," I said impatiently.

"Yeah, well… easy for you to say living with a hunk on a tropical island. Is your life amazing, or what? Oh my God… can you believe this? The same dickwad just cut me off again. *Motherfucker!*"

I heard the loud blaring sound of a car horn.

"You should come out and chillax with us," I said.

"Wouldn't that be nice? I think Mom's got dementia, and as always, my useless brother hasn't been any help."

"I'm sorry, Cassie."

"We finally closed on that house, and we're moving in like two weeks. The sellers wanted a fast close. *What was I thinking?*"

"Try doing that meditation cd that I sent you."

"If only I had time for that. Tequila shots work just fine!"

I gritted my teeth. I wanted to be supportive, but her incessant venting was getting on my nerves.

"Cassie, you have a loyal, loving husband and a beautiful baby. I don't know why it's always a half empty cup?"

"I just can't help it. Besides, I can say the same about you. Hot men always fall into your lap… *literally.* Jason was sexy, rich, and spoiled you like crazy."

"Yeah, well… look how that turned out."

I clenched and unclenched my free hand. *How could she not realize how miserable I was living a fake life in order to keep Jason happy? How I always put everyone first and silently suffered?* Cassie steamed ahead, oblivious to my comment. This was something we'd do in high school, compare our woes in a bizarre competition of whose life sucked the most. Cassie's laments about not having the latest, trendiest clothing and accessories used to annoy the hell out of Kailani and me.

"Now you're with an even sexier guy who would walk on cut glass for you. I mean… *really?*"

My face flushed with irritation. "Things aren't perfect, Cassie. He wants to move to Arizona for a lucrative job overseeing a clinic. *Arizona!*"

"Oh my God… it's hotter than hell there. Steve wanted us to move there to be closer to his grandparents. I said no way. Plus, you know… rattlesnakes!"

My throat tightened and I choked out, "My life isn't perfect, Cassie. It's far from it. I shouldn't have pushed him to come here... things are falling apart." Fresh tears stung my eyes.

"*Sweetie,*" Cassie sighed. "Whenever I'd get stressed, my mother would make me a cup of chamomile tea and say: *Breathe, mi corazon… just breathe.*"

Sometimes Cassie could surprise me. Just when I was ready to write her off—she says something comforting.

"I wish I could give you a big hug," Cassie added.

I inhaled a long, ragged breath. "You're the one with the perfect life," I said.

Before Cassie could respond, the call abruptly ended. I looked down at my phone and saw I had zero bars.

***

I saw Nakoa sitting on the bench at Lookout Point. I paused and studied his handsome profile. An aura of calmness radiated off him, and I felt hesitant to interrupt, but he turned his head and smiled.

"Come sit, sister."

"Sorry to interrupt."

He beckoned me forward. When I sat down, he leaned over and patted my hand. "What's troubling you?"

"Where do I begin?" I joked.

"I know your man is upset with you."

Tears pricked my eyes at his words. I bowed my head and brushed away a stray tear.

"*It will pass,*" Nakoa said calmly.

A flicker of hope swept through me. I wanted more reassurance, and I started to ask Nakoa a question, but he gently interrupted me.

"Why did you move to the islands?"

His question caught me off guard. "For a calmer, simpler life."

"And… *what else?*"

My mind went blank. I felt like I was taking a school pop-quiz and failing to find the right answer.

"To be with the *mother,*" Nakoa offered. He waved his hand to encompass the pristine, rippling ocean in front of us. "She summoned you here, and you heard her call. Her love is all around us. She wants you to embrace it *all*. We are here to love her back and be with her. You have to be willing to receive it."

"I don't know how to do that." I tucked my legs into my chest and hugged my knees close. My eyes welled up again. Despite the fact that Nakoa was right next to me, a feeling of loneliness swept over me.

He smiled. "Sister, you have all you need inside of you. Close your eyes and breathe into your heart. You will feel her." He leaned over and placed his hand on my shoulder. "She is waiting for you."

He got up and patted my hand in a comforting gesture and slipped away tacitly.

I felt a soft breeze on my face like a loving caress. The ocean waves crashed loudly against the jagged, slate-gray rocks below. Frothy white ocean water churned around the rocks as the waves receded. The crescent citrine sun dipped into the darkening horizon, its rays coloring the turquoise sky with streaks of coral pink and ochre. A peacefulness settled over me, and I knew the Mother was reaching out to me with a gift of presence and beauty.

My heart squeezed with gratitude.

Chapter Thirteen

The pleasing scent of jasmine perfumed the night air as I made my way to the yoga yurt. As I got closer, I saw the yurt glowing with amber light. It was a dramatic vision against the inky black night. The murmuring of soft voices came from inside the tent and slowed my steps. My palms were damp from nervousness. I ran my hands down the front of my yoga pants and looked up at the rose colored full moon, which added an air of mystery and magic to the setting. A sense of peace swept through me. Behind me, a familiar voice called out, and I was surprised to see Braydon.

"Hey, love!" he sang out.

"You're back."

He nodded with a grin as he slung his arm around my shoulders. "We pulled up about an hour ago. We had a blast."

So… Rodrigo is back too? The realization made me want to turn around, race back to the cabin, and ditch the meditation. As if reading my mind, Braydon gently put his hand on my back and propelled me forward toward the yurt.

"He and Lono are in town having dinner. I'm sure you two will have a lot to catch up on… *later.*"

We were at the wooden steps leading up to the yurt and he grabbed my hand and led me inside. The musky smell of incense greeted us, and I was surprised to see how full the room was. About twenty people sat quietly, cross-legged, facing the wooden altar. A white, ceramic Kwan Yin statue was the centerpiece. Dark pink dendrobium orchid flower buds were scattered at her feet, along with delicate seashells and polished rounds of pink quartz crystals. Surrounding Kwan Yin were flickering white votive candles, which threw shadows across her face, imbuing her with a contemplative expression. A white Gardenia flower floated in a small glass bowl of water. Soft flute music filtered in through the sound system, creating an even more tranquil setting. The wooden harmonium organ had been moved to the front row facing the altar. Braydon made his way to the front, while I hung back near the door. I wanted to leave quickly to see Rodrigo after the ceremony was over. *Would he come here later?* My heart leapt at the possibility that he'd show up. I glanced at the door expectantly. Conveniently, there was a plastic white folding chair next to the door. I sat down and drank in the mystical ambience.

Shara appeared, carrying her white crystal singing bowl, and took a seat near Braydon. Kailani made her way behind the harmonium and sat down on a round meditation pillow. The flute music stopped, and I watched as Shara gently circled the rubber mallet around the sides of the bowl, generating a soothing hum.

"Please take a deep breath in, hold, and gently release. Repeat three times," Shara instructed.

I closed my eyes, settled back in my chair, and drew in a deep breath. My shoulders dropped as I let out a long exhale.

"Together, we are on a journey to embrace the Mother." Shara said softly. "Let's be present and let any unnecessary thoughts float away. On the inhale, breathe in golden light. On the exhale, release any doubts or worries."

The calming drone of the harmonium filled the room, and I realized Shara had stopped playing the singing bowl.

"Place your hands palms up on your knees. This is to let Mother know you are ready to receive her."

The warmth inside the yurt and the droning organ music began to make me drowsy. I straightened up in my chair to rouse myself.

Shara said softly, "Can you feel her loving presence?"

The room began to spin, and I felt a *whoosh* as the yurt walls began to vibrate.

"You are safe, you are loved…*all is well*," Shara whispered.

My head dropped to my chest as an overwhelming fatigue enveloped me. In the dream, I was standing on a sun drenched beach facing the ocean. I saw a humpback whale breach over the water in an amazing, gravity-defying arc. My mouth fell open, and I rushed over to get a better view. The whale was gone, but I saw a little girl swimming happily—a golden aura emanated from her. She looked right at me and smiled, seeming familiar.

A sea turtle popped up next to her, and she laughed with delight and whispered, *"Lono!"*

Now I was really confused—was she related to Lono? Who was this little girl? Why was Lono popping up? Before I could even process the moment, the girl hopped on Lono's back, and they dove under the waves. I looked up to see a giant tidal wave coming at me and realized I didn't have time to get away—*I'm going to drown.*

***

I woke up to find myself alone inside the yurt. My mouth was dry and my eyes were itchy. The votive candles were burning low, and I wondered how long I'd been asleep.

I slowly got up and went to the door, the coqui frogs going full force, their familiar croaking felt oddly reassuring as I made my way down the dimly lit foot path. I wondered if Rodrigo was home yet. The thought of him being back made me hasten my steps, and I arrived breathlessly at our cabin door, pushing it open and calling out his name. *"Rodrigo?"*

There was only silence. I kicked my flip flops off and placed them beside the front door, then went into the bedroom and sat down heavily, my shoulders hunched over in disappointment. Maybe Rodrigo decided to stay with Lono? I heard the front door open and sat up. A moment later, Rodrigo stood framed in the bedroom doorway, clad only in a towel wrapped around his waist. My breath caught in my throat as my pulse raced rapidly.

"Nothing like a cold shower," he quipped.

"You're back," I blurted awkwardly.

A mix of emotions swirled inside me—relief, giddiness, and uncertainty. I wasn't sure what else to say.

"I guess we should talk," I said finally.

He took a step toward me. "Who wants to talk?" He cupped my face in his hands and leaned in for a lingering kiss. A liquid heat fanned out over my body.

"This is unexpected," I gasped.

"No more talking," he whispered, leaning over and kissing me again. I shut my eyes and enjoyed this unexpected moment. The towel didn't stay on very long.

***

There was nothing better than make-up sex. I curled up against Rodrigo and inhaled his fresh, soapy scent and the smoothness of his tanned skin. The tension that had gripped me for days melted away with each of his caresses. A lightness enveloped me as Rodrigo reached for my hand and threaded his fingers through mine.

"I guess we should talk about the elephant in the room?" I asked.

"You mean the *shark* in the room?" Rodrigo corrected.

"I'm sorry I kept it from you."

"I know. I talked to Lono and Braydon a lot about the situation."

"What'd they say?"

"Well, Lono jumped into the ocean and turned into a sea turtle… so, there's *that*."

My hand flew to my mouth with amusement. "Oh my God. How did Braydon react?"

"He laughed. For a moment, I thought he was going to turn into something and I was going to be the odd man out. Thankfully, that didn't happen. I guess everyone is a shapeshifter, including Kailani. Boy, do I feel like a dolt."

"Why? We were born like this… I didn't choose to be a shark. I didn't even know until I reconnected with Kailani. She never even mentioned she was a crow in all the time we've been friends. I just found out about a year ago!"

"Okay, I don't feel so bad."

"Why would you?"

"Look, you spent some time with my mother. From the outside, she's this airy-fairy… harmless earth mama. She wears crystals, communes with nature spirits, and sells organic herb tea. She tried to be a good mother but didn't fit in with the other mothers. She was even a Deadhead for a while."

"*Deadhead?*"

"You know… the *Grateful Dead.* She almost had a nervous breakdown when Jerry Garcia died. She didn't get out of bed for days, and when she did… she was like a zombie. I had to make food for both of us—we ate a lot of top ramen and grilled cheese sandwiches."

"I'm so sorry. That sounds rough."

"Then my parents split up, and they were the first to get divorced in the neighborhood. I was kinda glad they did because they were fighting all the time anyway. It was a lonely time—I didn't have anyone to talk to."

"I understand. People thought it was weird that it was only Aunt Lily and me. It seemed like all the other kids had parents who did things with them. I never learned to ride a bike or how to swim."

He sighed. "The only thing that saved me was I was good at baseball and had decent grades."

"You played baseball?"

"Yep. Pitcher… a damn good one. Plus my batting average was three fifty."

"*Really*? That's pretty good!"

"You're into baseball?"

"Jason was a big Giants fan, so we had seasons tickets."

I inwardly cringed—I said the "J" word again. Even worse, I doubt Rodrigo ever sat in box seats like we used to.

"I hardly went to the games. It was mostly for VIP restaurant customers," I added lamely.

Rodrigo stroked my hair. "I can't afford box seats, but you won't have to work if I get that job in Arizona."

"I'm sorry I wasn't supportive about your job offer."

"And… I'm sorry I freaked out over your mano reveal. I'm sure it wasn't easy to tell me. I guess your fears came true when I took off with Lono and Braydon."

I nodded. "It was a tough few days."

"It triggered me because it reminded me of how my mother dumped stuff on me at the last minute. Like… *son, your father and I have decided you need to live with Aunt Rosa while we figure things out.* Out of the blue, I had to pack up and move across town to live with Dad's sister and her bratty kids. Aunt Rosa never liked Mom, and she'd bitch all day about my crazy, hippy-dippy mother. My cousins weren't any better. I didn't even have an actual bed, I had to sleep on a smelly, fold-out sofa in the basement."

"That's awful."

"I had to constantly listen to my aunt complain how my mom was turning my dad into an alcoholic. How my mom's infidelities brought shame on the family… it just kept going on and on."

"That must have been so hard. I'm sorry that happened."

"Now you can understand why I don't like being ambushed with bad news. Not that being part shark is bad."

"I get it. That's why you want the job in Arizona, so we can afford a nice home."

He nodded with a smirk. "A place of our own with *indoor plumbing.*"

I poked him playfully. "You said you liked the outdoor shower."

"Well… I lied."

"I told Cassie about Arizona, and she said besides the stifling heat… there's rattlesnakes!"

Rodrigo laughed and shook his head. *"Come on!"*

"It's a big company, right? Don't they have any openings in California?"

"Possibly. But not as a clinic director… it won't necessarily be forever. We can figure this out together. I know you want to be able to jump on a plane to visit Kailani and Shara."

"Promise me… if there's ever an opportunity back in California, you'll consider it."

"I promise."

"One last thing… are you sure you don't want kids?"

I heard the surprise in his voice. "What's this about? We already talked about this."

"I know, but you're still young, if you change your mind later…"

"I'm pushing *forty*. Having a bunch of kids was never on my bucket list." He leaned over and kissed the top of my head. "Being with an amazing, loving, and hot woman was *always* on my bucket list."

"Even if she has fish gills?"

Rodrigo grinned. "Definitely."

Chapter Fourteen

The tantalizing smell of sizzling bacon woke me up, along with the noise of dishes clattering in the sink. I heard Rodrigo humming cheerfully as he moved around the kitchen. I forked my fingers through my hair and slid out of bed. Rodrigo had set the table with plates, paper napkins, and forks. A stack of buttered blueberry pancakes rested on a big dinner plate in the center of the dining table.

"Hey, sleepyhead!" Rodrigo greeted me with a kiss on my forehead.

"It smells incredible in here," I replied.

I moved to the kitchen sink and reached for my toothbrush. Rodrigo grabbed two ceramic mugs and filled them with coffee from a glass French press coffeemaker. I rinsed my mouth out with tap water from the sink, then sat down at the table. Rodrigo put down a mug of coffee in front of me. A swirl of cream floated on top. I took a sip and sighed happily. He placed two pancakes in front of me with three pieces of bacon.

"This is just like the old days at Lulu's place," I said.

"That seems so long ago."

Rodrigo placed a glass bottle of maple syrup in front of me. I twisted the cap off and drizzled some syrup over the pancakes as he sat across from me, cupping his coffee mug between his palms. His eyes were bright, and he flashed his trademark irresistible smile at me.

"*What?*" I asked.

I stuck a piece of bacon in my mouth and almost swooned at the crunchy, fatty deliciousness. I could never be a vegetarian!

"So, I got a call from the job recruiter about that job in Arizona."

"Oh?"

"He said the company wants to move forward with an in-person interview. In fact, they want me to meet the CEO and COO in person at the corporate headquarters in San Francisco. They're paying to fly me out and set me up in their corporate apartment."

"Wait… you're interviewing for the job in Arizona, right? But you have to interview in San Francisco at the company headquarters?"

Rodrigo nodded. He was tapping his foot impatiently under the table. "They have clinics all over the west coast."

"So, when's all this happening?"

"They want me to fly out this weekend for a Monday meeting. I want you to come with me. We could make it a little vacation."

A nervous fluttering started in my stomach. My mouth felt arid, so I took a healthy swig and nearly burned my mouth.

"It's happening so fast."

He reached over and grabbed my hand. "This is an amazing opportunity. I didn't think it would happen this quickly either."

"I guess they're serious."

"The HR manager said the salary would be six figures."

"You talked about money already?"

"He brought it up. Also, fully paid medical and dental, and get this… *three weeks of pto right off the bat.*"

"So, we'd fly out… like, on Sunday?"

"Or Saturday. I have to get back to the HR guy to confirm."

I didn't know what to say. I could see how enthusiastic he was, so I just nodded. Rodrigo lifted my hand and kissed my palm tenderly

"Then you should call him and let him know we'll be there."

I wished I could be happy for him. Instead, a dull ache formed in the pit of my stomach as anxious thoughts of packing up and relocating swirled in my mind. A jab of sadness pricked at me when I imagined leaving the lodge and my friends. Yet I owed it to Rodrigo to keep an open mind. I just couldn't shake the forlorn feeling of being abruptly uprooted by fate.

***

I offered to tidy up the kitchen, but Rodrigo insisted he'd clean. I decided to walk over to the lodge kitchen and see if Kailani was around. I needed her sage presence to help process Rodrigo's sudden news. As I got close to the kitchen, I saw Nakoa park his truck in front of the lodge. He greeted me with a warm smile and a wave.

"Aloha, sister."

"We're out of eggs, so your timing is perfect. Did Shara call you?"

He tapped the side of his head. "The ancestors told me to come today."

I helped him unload crates of fresh eggs and pushed the kitchen door open with my foot. I offered him some iced tea, which he gratefully accepted. We sat down at the long, wooden dining table. He sipped his tea tacitly, and we enjoyed a brief companionable moment of silence. I always felt relaxed in his calm presence. He turned to me and raised his eyebrows.

"What is going on with you, sister?"

I sighed. "We might be moving back to the states."

He nodded. "I saw Rodrigo yesterday, and he said he'd had an interview. He seems excited."

"He's ready to go back, but I wish I could stay here forever." My voice faltered, and Nakoa reached over and gently put his hand over mine.

"The ancestors have gifted you with their presence and wisdom. Perhaps you are meant to share it with others back on the continent."

I smiled at his kind words. The image of Cassie rushing around with her kids popped into my mind.

"I don't think people on the continent really care about their wisdom. People are too consumed by their own busyness to pay attention."

"That might be so, but there are some who are hungry for spiritual wisdom. Perhaps you are meant to spread some aloha back in California?"

"You mean like an aloha ambassador?" I joked. "I don't think I'm qualified."

"Of course you are. You radiate genuine goodwill and love. You don't give yourself enough credit, sister."

"Story of my life," I sighed.

***

I should have felt warm and fuzzy in the lodge kitchen surrounded by Shara, Kailani and Nakoa. Everyone was congratulating Rodrigo on his job news. We sat over a delicious dinner of Shara's famous Shakshuka, spinach salad with pecans, cranberries, and goat cheese and *poi* dinner rolls. It felt festive and pleasant, except for the depressing realization that pretty soon, this chapter of my life was ending. Rodrigo patted my knee under the dining table and leaned over to plant a quick kiss on my cheek. I smiled wanly. They were talking about the company apartment that Rodrigo's new potential employer had booked for us.

"It's in the Marina, near where my mom is housesitting." Rodrigo said with a grin.

"I love that area!" Kailani said

"It was meant to be!" Shara said cheerfully.

"Wait. Margot said she was housesitting in the Mission," I said.

"Maybe she got confused. She texted me to invite us to stay with her in the Marina."

"Well, she texted me pictures of a place in the Mission."

He shrugged. "It doesn't matter since we've got our own apartment in the Marina. Anyway, Mom is going to take Noelani wedding dress shopping. She knows of some cool places in the Haight."

"The Haight was her old stomping grounds," I said.

"I have fond memories of that neighborhood also," Nakoa said.

We all turned to him in surprise.

"You used to live there?" I asked.

He grinned. "*Briefly.* There was a lovely woman who enticed me there."

"*Nakoa!*" Kailani exclaimed. "We want details."

He shook his head. "Some things are private."

"You are full of surprises," Shara remarked.

He shook his head with a smile. "This kapuna must maintain an air of mystery." He chuckled, then he raised his glass to toast us. "Many blessings to this beautiful couple."

We all clinked our frosty glasses.

Why can't I be happy for us? Why do I feel like I'm being betrayed because Kailani isn't going to miss me as much as I'm going to miss her?

Kailani stood to clear the dishes, and I got up to help her. Rodrigo, Shara, and Nakoa continued to chat amiably while we piled up the ceramic plates and salad bowl. Kailani led the way to the sink and began to run some water.

Before I could say anything, she turned to me. "I know you're sad about leaving, but this is a great opportunity for him."

"I get that. I finally felt settled here, and now we're leaving. Remember the first day of school when you're nervous and unsure? That's how I feel."

"It's not like you're moving to a foreign country. You know San Francisco like the back of your hand. You guys will do great—it's a fresh start. You're building a life together."

I felt a sting of disappointment at her well-meaning words.

"Aren't you going to miss me?"

Kailani leaned forward and hugged me. "*Of course I am!*"

My throat tightened, and I felt tears forming.

"Shara and I will come visit. And… you know you'll always have a home here at the lodge."

I sucked in a shaky breath to settle myself. I didn't want to ruin the festive energy of tonight's gathering.

"Come help me serve up this lemon blueberry bread," Kailani said with a smile. Then she patted my back. "Try to be happy for Rodrigo—he needs you to be onboard."

I know she meant it kindly, but a bubble of resentment formed in my stomach. *Of course I want to support Rodrigo.* But Kailani was *my* friend and I needed her to understand how hard it was for me to just pack up and leave. As Kailani washed the dinner dishes, I went to the counter and sliced up the bread and placed them on a dinner plate. I decided to set aside my feelings and to enjoy Rodrigo's moment. When I turned back to the table, Nakoa waved me over to sit. I put the plate down in the center of the table.

"Nakoa wants us to do a ho'oponopono ceremony before we get married." Rodrigo said.

"I'm not sure what that means?"

"It would be good medicine for you to come together and receive each other before you get married." Nakoa explained.

"Kailani and I did this before we got married too. It was very healing." Shara said.

I looked at Rodrigo who was already eating his second slice of lemon bread.

"It's up to you." Rodrigo said.

It felt like the right thing to do. "Thank you Nakoa." I said.

***

As we walked back to our cabin, I marveled at the brilliant, inky night sky. The stars shone brilliantly, like diamond dust. The chirping of coqui frogs filled the humid, damp air. A sudden cool breeze was refreshing.

"The stars are amazing here."

"No light pollution, so you can see them clearly," Rodrigo replied.

"I'm going to miss all of this," I sighed.

"You can always come back. I know Kailani will really miss you."

"She doesn't act like it."

Rodrigo took my hand. "Maybe she doesn't show it, but she will. I know this is tough for you. Let's try it for a year, and if you're not happy, we'll come back."

I looked I into his eyes and saw his sincerity. My chest swelled with gratitude at his loving words.

He took both my hands and squeezed them. "I know this is important to you. *I love you.*"

We got to the cabin and kicked off our flip flops onto the porch. Rodrigo opened the door for me, and I looked around at the cozy space we'd called home for the past year. Tears welled in my eyes, both for the peaceful sanctuary it had provided and the fact that soon this sojourn would be a memory.

Chapter Fifteen

"You look like Stevie Nicks." I said.

Margot smiled shyly. "That's a huge compliment. She was my idol for a long time. So talented and beautiful. *Still beautiful,*" Margot sighed.

We'd taken an Uber to 710 Ashbury Street, where the Grateful Dead had once lived. Margot jumped out of the car excitedly and stood in front of the Victorian house reverently. She clasped her hands in front of her and closed her eyes. Today, she wore a black, velvet newsboy cap slung low over her eyes. She had on a black, fringed lacy shawl over a long v-neck denim dress and red and black, leather cowgirl boots. I felt frumpy and uninspired walking with her. I had my default outfit of a cotton t-shirt over leggings, running shoes and a fleece jacket.

"I was just a girl the last time I was here." Margot sighed.

I stood back and waited patiently as she reveled in her memories. The ornate brown and tan Victorian façade was immaculately maintained. The peaked door lintel was festooned with a gold painted filigree design and framed two dark, wood, carved doors. There was a black, wrought iron gate tipped with gold paint in front of the stone steps. After a few minutes, she suggested we walk around. The morning had started off foggy and damp, and

I already missed our sunny island idyll. The idea of moving back to the states depressed me.

Margot put a hand on my shoulder and looked at me with concern. "What's wrong? I can feel your energy is off."

I shrugged. "Even though it's only been a year, it feels weird to be back."

"You have a wonderful life in Hawaii with your besties."

I nodded. "It's not so much moving back as much as having to leave. I know this is a great opportunity for Rodrigo, though."

"But… *is this what you want?*"

I shrugged and turned away from Margot. "I want him to be happy. He wants to build a life together, and he loves his work. I could tell he was getting bored in Hawaii."

I didn't sound convincing, and Margot let my remark pass. I zipped up my fleece jacket and stuck both hands into my pockets. She gestured toward Gus's Community Market nearby. "Let's get something hot to drink."

Gus's Community Market was a forest-green building topped by a bright mural of farmers tilling verdant farmland. The market was next door to the crimson Jimi Hendrix Red Store building.

Margot gestured at an empty table inside the sidewalk parklet. "Save us a table. I'll get the coffees."

I reached for my wallet, and she waved me off with a smile. The parklets sprang up during Covid, and most restaurants and cafes kept them as additional outside seating. The fog had started to dissipate, and rays of cheery sunlight brightened the neighborhood. I looked around and true to its free-spirited and bohemian roots of The Haight saw many colorfully dressed and unusual people. A young woman with canary-yellow cropped hair dressed in an orange jumpsuit sauntered by, chatting amiably on her cell phone. What a contrast to the island life I'd enjoyed over the past year. I felt a jab of sadness at the thought of leaving Hawaii and returning to the busyness of California.

Margot returned with two paper cups of coffee and placed them on the black metal table in front of me.

"I think you like a little cream in yours?" she asked.

I nodded, then took the plastic lid off and blew on the coffee. "Smells good."

"What were you thinking about? You seemed deep in thought."

"Nakoa called me an aloha ambassador."

"Absolutely! You embody the island's aloha spirit. I love getting to know you, and I'm thrilled you're going to be part of the family."

"Thank you, Margot. You're so sweet to say that."

She shook her head at me. "Not at all. I'm being truthful. You've enchanted my son, and he's a tough customer. You're the first woman he's totally trusted."

A ripple of happiness swept through me. "Really?"

Margot winked at me playfully. "Really."

Her words perked me up. I sipped my coffee slowly, inhaling the fresh, smoky aroma of the dark, coffee bean roast. Rodrigo would enjoy this blend.

"That Nakoa is gorgeous. Do you know if he's single?"

I shook my head. "He keeps his cards close to the vest." I quipped.

"He's got such intense, sexy energy. I wonder what it'd be like to be with him?" Margot's face softened into a dreamy expression. I almost laughed because she seemed more like a teenager than a seventy year old senior. Did Margot know that Nakoa was a shapeshifter? I decided not to bring it up unless she mentioned it.

Margot looked around us with a bemused smile.

"I'm sure The Haight has changed a lot since over the years, hasn't it?"

Margot sighed wistfully. "That's the nature of life, isn't it? Constant change."

"I bet it was an interesting time growing up around here back in the day."

"It was. Between the Vietnam war and vibrant music scene, it was really something. The Grateful Dead had such an impact on me."

"In what way?"

"I grew up in such a strict household. When I went to my first concert, I was blown away by how alive the music was. I felt like I found my people." Margot chuckled. "Sounds silly, I know."

"I think a lot of people feel like they don't fit with their family of origin. I totally get it."

"My mother said I was a hopeless dreamer. I wanted to travel the world and meet lots of different people. She had a hard life after my father left. It was just the two of us."

"What happened to your father? Rodrigo never talks about his grandparents." My interest was piqued. He tended to change the subject when it came to either sets of grandparents. I hadn't pursued the topic because of his reticence.

Margot shrugged. "He went to work as usual one day and just never came back. We moved in with my grandmother for a while. It was tough."

"So, your mother never remarried?"

"No. She was incredibly bitter, and I vowed I wouldn't end up like that."

"So, you bought an RV and hit the road!"

"*I wish.* I thought about it."

"I thought you said you sold your Miata for an RV? Did I misunderstand?"

"My ex-husband had a RV for a time—maybe I said *that*?"

Margot smiled at my confusion. I was certain she'd mentioned the RV previously but let it go.

I got a beep on my phone and looked down to see that Rodrigo had texted. "His interview is done. He wants to know if we could meet up for lunch and where."

"That was a long interview. I guess that's good news, right?" She looked hopeful. I knew she was thrilled at the possibility we might be living close by again. I tried not to think about it.

"Well, he texted a laughing emoji… so I guess that's good."

"I'd like to go to one more store before we leave for lunch."

"Sure. I'll tell him we'll meet up in about an hour? Is that okay?"

"Perfect."

***

The store was called Love of Ganesh, and it was a tightly packed trinket store full of crystals and Buddhist demi-god statues of different deities. I carefully navigated around the tables laden with crystals, jewelry, and clothing. The strong smell of sandalwood incense pervaded the cramped boutique. Margot was in her element, sifting through trays of multi-colored crystals. I felt a little claustrophobic as I shuffled between tables teeming with minerals. When I looked up, a poster caught my eye of an aqua-blue Hawaiian maiden with swirls of thick, matching blue hair and a necklace of seashells.

"Lovely, isn't she?"

I turned to see a bespeckled, petite Indian woman beside me. She had on a t-shirt with Love of Ganesh emblazoned across the chest.

"You work here?" I asked.

She nodded. "That is an artist's rendering of the Mo'o. They're like nature spirits that protect the freshwater ponds in Hawaii."

I made a mental note to ask Nakoa or Lono about the Mo'o.

"They're said to be able to shapeshift from beautiful women into ferocious dragons."

Shapeshifters!

"Good to know," I joked.

"Of course, it's all mythology. There aren't really any shapeshifters."

I tried not to laugh. "Of course not."

"You're from Hawaii… aren't you? You give off those island vibes!" She peered intently at me over her glasses.

"She's an aloha ambassador!" Margot said behind me. She put her arm around my shoulders fondly. "This is my future daughter-in-law. She's moving back after she gets married."

"Congratulations. I wish you many blessings!" She put her hands together in a prayer and bowed her head.

"Thank you."

I was touched by her kind, spontaneous gesture.

Margot grinned at me. "It's all meant to be!" she declared.

***

Pier 39 was the last place I wanted to be. The original plan was to meet Rodrigo at Fort Mason for a vegetarian lunch at Greens Restaurant. However, along the way, Margot felt a migraine coming on and decided to go back to her housesitting place at the marina. I went on to meet Rodrigo at Pier 39. The Uber dropped me off at the SkyStar Ferris Wheel. Rodrigo was already standing in front. I couldn't believe how handsome he looked in his wool, gray, checked Hugo Boss suit. His outfit was impeccably accessorized with a black and white striped, silk tie and a crisply pressed white shirt. He had on his usual black aviator sunglasses, which seriously added to his hotness.

"Wow. You clean up pretty good!" I said.

"Ya think?"

"Why'd you want to meet here?"

"My dad used to take me here to eat seafood and look at the sea lions. Fond memories." He leaned over and kissed my forehead. "I always wanted to bring a date here but never got the chance."

"It's so… *touristy.*"

"I know!" He grabbed my hand and flashed his irresistible boyish grin. My heart fluttered.

"Jason brought me here once to look at a restaurant he wanted to buy. It didn't pan out, though."

I clamped my mouth shut and my cheeks burned with embarrassment. I had twenty years of memories to unwind. Sometimes it was hard for me not to randomly blurt out snippets from my past. For a while, Rodrigo had referred to my ex-husband as "the *dickwad.*" I checked his reaction, but he was lost in his sentimental memories as we moved through throngs of bustling tourists. The inviting smell of sugar treats infused the air as we walked past a cart festooned with plastic bags of cotton candy, funnel cakes, and caramel popcorn. Rodrigo stood out in his formal attire, but it made my chest swell with pride that I was with such a sexy, goodlooking man.

We found our way to Swiss Louis, the Italian restaurant he and his father used eat at. The restaurant was palatial, with white tablecloths and waterfront views of the ocean. We got a window seat overlooking the sea lion habitat. Their loud, husky barking was audible through the large, closed windows. I looked down at their corpulent, chestnut-brown bodies lounging lazily on the pier. They were huge and weren't as cute and cuddly looking as local harbor seals.

"Nothing's changed," Rodrigo said happily. He had a childlike glow about him as he stared out the window, marveling at them.

"Hey, didn't you say your mother traveled around in a RV?"

He nodded and turned back to me with a puzzled look.

"She sold her car to buy it. She mentioned it at the restaurant, remember?"

"I know. I brought it up when we were in the Haight, and she denied ever owning one."

"She must have been confused." He shook his head dismissively. "I don't think it's a big deal. She's always been a little forgetful."

"When was the last time she had a full check up at the doctors?"

He shrugged. "She doesn't believe in doctors."

"I just think she should get checked out. Shara might know a good neurologist."

Rodrigo sighed. "That's the last thing I'd bring up with my mom."

I decided to let it go and changed the subject. "How'd the interview go?"

He grinned. "They're emailing me an offer letter."

"Really… so quick?"

He nodded. "Even better news… they just got an opening for a senior therapist here in the city. The director of the clinic here is retiring in three months, and they said if I could wait, I could slide into that job. They asked if I could start working in two weeks?"

Two weeks! My heart sank as visions of leaving Kailani, Shara, and Lono flashed before me. No more turtle swimming with Lono, no more of Shara's delicious baked goodies, and no more bonding with Kailani over iced tea in the lodge kitchen at night.

Rodrigo noticed my expression and leaned over and put his hand over mine. "Of course, you can stay as long as you want until you're ready to move back. But isn't that great… we'll be here instead of Arizona."

I formed a smile and ignored the emptiness in the pit of my stomach. *This is really happening. I'll be leaving the islands.*

"What about the wedding?" I sputtered.

"They said I could start right away and go back to the Big Island for the wedding later. *Easy peasy!*"

He was so happy, I didn't want to spoil the moment by voicing my angst about leaving the islands.

"I had a great feeling about this interview. From the moment I walked in, it just flowed. We'll make a fresh start together as a married couple. Best day ever!"

It's really happening.

Chapter Sixteen

In the dream I was drifting through wispy, cream-colored clouds. The air caressed my face and hair tenderly. *This is so easy!* I marveled at how effortless it was to fly. I didn't even have to flap my arms, I just blissfully bobbed around like a leaf in the wind. Then I heard shouting, and my heart squeezed with fear. *What was that? Who's yelling? What's going on?*

I sat up with a start, my heart pounding wildly. My face was hot and sticky. I looked around for Rodrigo, but he wasn't beside me in bed. We'd only been back in Hawaii two days. Getting acclimated back at the lodge felt strange knowing we would be leaving soon. Part of me wanted to press a cosmic fast forward button so I would already be married and back in California and skip the goodbyes. I was terrible at parting ways with people and situations. I had even quit jobs and snuck out in order to not attend my own going away party.

I heard Rodrigo's voice on the porch and got up. A ripple of nervousness flashed through me at the terse sound of his voice. I walked through the kitchen and saw him standing on the porch in his boxer shorts. He looked tense as he paced back and forth on the wooden porch. His brow was furrowed in concentration, and he was clenching and unclenching his free hand as he held the cell phone in his other hand. When I stepped onto the porch, he ended the call and looked at me.

"What is it?" I asked.

"Braydon's missing."

"What do you mean missing?"

"That was Lono on the phone. He and Braydon were supposed to go swimming at Carlsmith this morning, and he didn't show up. He called Kailani, and she went to check his cabin, and his phone and keys were next to his bed. It looks like he wasn't there last night."

"Maybe he met someone? Yesterday at breakfast he was meeting friends at the ecstatic dance party down the road."

He shook his head. "Maybe. But Lono called some friends at the party, and they hadn't seen Braydon all evening."

My scalp prickled, and a disquieting feeling roiled in my stomach. Rodrigo nodded in the direction of the lodge.

"Lono's on his way here, and we're all going to meet to figure out what to do."

Rodrigo pushed past me to go inside. I followed him into the bedroom. We quickly got dressed in silence. I put on a lodge t-shirt and slipped into my yoga pants, while Rodrigo pulled on some running shorts. I was in a daze as we hurried to the front door.

Where is Braydon?

We walked quietly down the muddy, single track toward the lodge kitchen. The air was still chilly with a hint of moisture. Up ahead, I could see Lono's truck parked in front of the lodge. When we entered the kitchen, Kailani, Shara, and Lono stood around the long, wooden dining table talking softly. They looked up when Rodrigo and I stepped inside.

"Any news?" I asked hopefully.

Lono shook his head. "Nothing."

"When I went into his cabin, I noticed his cell phone and wallet on the nightstand," Kailani said.

"None of this makes any sense," Shara said.

The door opened abruptly, and Nakoa walked in. I immediately felt a shift in the room as he quietly took in the scene. His calm demeanor settled us all down.

"Something has happened," Nakoa said.

"Braydon's disappeared," I blurted.

"We're worried," Kailani chimed in.

Nakoa nodded and looked over at me. "Come with me."

"Where are you going?" Rodrigo asked.

"We will go to Braydon's cabin," Nakoa said.

"*Uncle*… Kailani already looked there," Shara said.

"Everyone… please wait here," Nakoa replied.

He walked purposely toward the kitchen door. I followed and glanced back at Rodrigo, who raised his eyebrows in confusion. Nakoa remained focused and silent as we walked toward the cabin. Within minutes, we were stepping onto the porch. Nakoa held the door open for me as I ducked inside. The modest room was neat and stark. The bed was neatly made up. Nakoa glanced around the small space as if tuning into something. Then he went to the nightstand

and picked up a bracelet. He handed it to me. It was a nice looking koa wood and copper band. The koa wood links were shaped like small arrowheads framed in a bronze-like finish. I looked up at Nakoa.

"What do you feel?" he asked.

I shook my head. "I'm not sure what you're asking."

He reached over and gently closed my fingers over the bracelet.

"There is energy in that bracelet—Braydon's energy. I think it will help us find him."

My palm began tingling, and I closed my eyes to concentrate. A ghostly image of Braydon appeared, and it was like watching a movie. He was looking up with a smile.

"What do you see?" Nakoa asked.

I shook my head. "I just see him smiling at something."

Nakoa put his hand over mine. The tingling in my palm increased. I saw Braydon reaching out to touch something. He was looking up at… a tree. I recognized the feathery, lavender foliage and realized it was a Jacaranda tree.

"I see a Jacaranda tree. He's touching it."

"Anything else?"

Nakoa's hand tightened slightly over mine, and the tingling increased again. I shook my head. He removed his hand, and I opened my eyes and blinked.

"What just happened?"

"I think you found our friend," Nakoa replied.

I started to put the bracelet back on the nightstand.

"Keep it for now. It will help us trace his steps."

***

We updated everyone at the lodge kitchen as we headed out to look for Braydon. Nakoa asked that everyone stay put in case Braydon came back. Then we drove down the road toward Turtle Beach in Nakoa's delivery truck. The truck cabin's immaculate interior was tan vinyl, with the gear shifter sticking out of the side of the steering wheel. I brushed my fingers across the clean dashboard as disquieting thoughts swirled through my mind. I remembered earlier how Braydon said how Namaka could summon him with her irresistible siren's call. A grisly image popped in my mind of him lying unconscious at the bottom of the narrow, craggy path. I knew he liked to meditate at Turtle Beach at dawn when it was deserted. *I hope you're okay, Braydon!* The windows were open, and humid air blew through my hair. Nakoa had been quiet once we climbed into the truck. He seemed focused on a specific destination.

"*There,*" Nakoa said.

I looked up as we neared an old, abandoned chapel. Beside the small church was a Jacaranda tree. The violet branches next to the weathered, white church façade made an interesting and colorful tableau. Nakoa drove past the tree about fifty yards and got out. I hastily followed as he marched toward a thick grove of hapu'u tree ferns. My bare legs brushed up against their delicate, feathery leaves as I tried to keep up with him. We descended down a steep slope in careful, mincing steps to avoid tripping on the uneven, narrow path, soon coming upon a hidden cove. I was surprised to see it after traversing through the dense foliage. Foamy, alabaster-tipped waves crashed loudly against tall, jagged, black boulders which encircled the cove. Nakoa abruptly stopped and shaded his eyes as he surveyed the rocky, black sand.

"Take out the bracelet."

I reached into my back pocket and pulled out the koa wood bracelet. It began to tingle in my palm again. He studied my face.

"So, he is here," Nakoa said.

I shook my head. "The tingling is faint. I feel like he's close by but not here."

"Can you tune in with your *mano* senses?"

"I don't know how."

He tapped the side of my neck gently. "Bring your gills out."

I closed my eyes and willed my gills to appear. I felt a soft rippling effect and reached up to touch them.

"Now… tune into the bracelet. What do you feel?"

I shook my head. "*Nothing.*"

Nakoa sighed in frustration and began to pace on the rocky black sand. I was letting both Nakoa and Braydon down, and my face burned with shame. I wanted to sink into the ground. My throat tightened. Then my gills began to ripple, and an image of Braydon flashed before me. I saw him curled up in a fetal position, sleeping on a dusty, wooden floor.

"He's in the church!" I yelled.

A look of surprise flashed across Nakoa's face. He grabbed my hand, and we hurried back up the path to his truck. He started the engine and turned the truck around, back toward the church. In minutes, we were pulling into the gravel driveway. Nakoa grabbed a bottle of water and handed it to me. The small chapel must have been lovely back in the day, with its steepled roof and white, carved double doors. Now the exterior was faded and the wood bleached by the relentless sun.

Nakoa pushed the door open, and a dank smell assaulted us. We stepped inside, and at the back of the church, we saw Braydon lying still on the dark, wood altar. I gasped in shock and stood transfixed at the sight. A large, arched, stained glass window illuminated the stark altar. A bright ray of sunlight seemed to encapsulate him in a gilded aura. The scene reminded me of the dream I'd had with the crow. I swallowed hard and tried to stop my hands from shaking. Nakoa rushed toward the altar and knelt down beside Braydon. He shook his arm lightly. To our relief, we heard Braydon moan softly.

"Wake up, boy," Nakoa said.

Braydon lifted his head and squinted groggily at us. "Where's *Namaka*?" he whispered.

Nakoa and I exchanged confused looks. Then he leaned over and slipped his arm around Braydon's shoulders, helping him up into a sitting position. I stepped forward with the water, and Nakoa uncapped the plastic bottle.

"Here… sip slowly."

Braydon took a dainty sip. "I saw her."

"*Namaka?*" Nakoa repeated. He looked over at me. "Pele's sister?"

Braydon nodded dazedly. "She led me here."

Then he looked around the chapel. "Where am I?"

"The old chapel," Nakoa replied.

Now it was Braydon who looked confused. "How did I get here?"

"That's what we'd like to know," I said.

Braydon shook his head vigorously as though clearing his mind. "I don't remember anything." He took a healthy swig of water and coughed. Nakoa put a steadying hand on his shoulder.

"Take it easy. When you feel ready, I'll help you up."

Braydon nodded meekly. "All I remember is that Namaka summoned me."

Nakoa and I glanced uneasily at each other again. He helped Braydon awkwardly stand and kept his arm around Braydon's waist to steady him.

When we stepped out into the sunlight, Braydon shaded his eyes and sighed. "I wish I knew what happened to me," he said.

"We'll figure this out later. Right now, let's get you back to the lodge," I said.

I turned back and glanced at the arched window one last time before I closed the door. My scalp tingled, and a strange shivering feeling rippled through me.

I have been here before, a long time ago.

Chapter Seventeen

"I hate how he just jumps in and rips through the waves. He makes it look so easy," Braydon said.

Braydon seemed to have recovered from his strange, paranormal experience. He still had no memory of how he'd ended up at the church. However, we were all thankful he was doing well. Lono, Braydon, and I decided to take a drive to Carlsmith Beach. Braydon and I watched Lono body surfing effortlessly.

"Well, he is a turtle," I said,

"I never thanked you and Nakoa for rescuing me."

"It was a team effort."

"But you tuned in and found me. That was hella awesome."

"Thanks to Nakoa. He kind of orchestrated the whole thing."

"You okay? You seem a little distracted today." Braydon looked at me with concern. It was hard not to be hypnotized by his deep, ocean-blue eyes.

"That chapel… I've been there before. I've had this recurring dream about it."

"You mean, like, in a past life?"

I nodded. The memory of the stained, arched window still gave me chills.

Braydon lightly ran his fingertips over my arm. "Chicken skin," he teased.

"Something happened at that chapel a long time ago, and I was there."

"You mean… like, someone got killed?"

I shook my head. "I don't know."

Off in the distance, Lono floated contentedly on the waves in his turtle form.

Excited shouting drew my attention to a group of tourists, laughing and pointing toward the water where Lono was swimming. They looked like college students on spring break. Two young men waded into the water, getting unnervingly close to Lono with their cell phones, ready to snap a photo. Braydon sprang up and rushed over toward them, waving his arms to catch their attention.

"Hey guys… it's illegal to harass the turtles!" he yelled.

The men were startled. A young woman with the group stepped forward. "We just want to take some pictures. We're not going to hurt him," she said.

Braydon clenched his jaw and fisted his hands on his hips. "You have to allow at least ten feet. The *honus* are considered sacred to the Hawaiians—please respect that. And no sneaking out at night to get a selfie with a *honu* and blinding them."

The group looked at each other with a mix of confusion and embarrassment. The men waded out of the water. They left grumbling.

Braydon shook his head. "Don't forget to use reef safe sunscreen. Protect the reefs!"

"You're on the war path," I teased.

"Babe, I'm a total *wahine koa* when I need to be. Besides, sunscreen is a scam. I never use it and I have perfect skin."

"Yes, you do!"

"Vitamin D is nature's miracle healer. Sit in the sun first thing in the morning and you're good."

Lono emerged from the ocean in his human form. I handed him a large, white, lodge towel, which he accepted with a smile.

"Hey, *brah*… thanks for looking out for me," Lono said.

Lono and Braydon bumped fists.

"Always, *brah*," Braydon said.

Lono plopped down next to us.

"Braydon gave those tourists a talking to!" I said.

"They needed to be seriously schooled," Braydon replied.

"People need to be more respectful," Lono agreed.

"Where's your man?" Lono asked. "Doesn't Rodrigo leave tomorrow for the continent?"

I tried to ignore the tightness in my gut. I didn't want to think about the drive to the airport to drop Rodrigo off. I was torn between going with him and staying longer at the lodge with Kailani and Shara. I absently twisted my engagement ring around my finger.

"He starts work on Monday, and he'll have ten-hour days learning the job. He told me to stay and enjoy myself."

"I know Kailani will miss you. *I'll miss you too!*" Lono said. He leaned over and jiggled my bare foot fondly.

"Is Nakoa doing the ho'oponopono ceremony tonight?" Braydon asked.

I nodded. "There's a lot going on all at once." My stomach knotted up. I had wanted to spend the evening alone with Rodrigo, but Nakoa was leaving to visit relatives in Las Vegas and wouldn't be back until our wedding. Rodrigo didn't want to wait.

"The ceremony is a blessing to start your new life together," Lono said.

"Did you talk to Kailani about it? She said it was a healing experience," he added.

"I'm sure it'll be fine," I said quickly.

Lono and Braydon gave me reassuring smiles. I knew they didn't really understand my nervousness. I wasn't sure I understood it either.

***

I walked toward the meditation yurt in the darkness. The coqui frogs were going full blast, and I felt a pang of sadness that soon all this would be a memory. Ahead of me, the yurt glowed softly with ambient light. A light breeze jostled the tent flaps. I kicked off my sandals at the entrance and peeked inside. Nakoa was sitting cross-legged in silent meditation. Before him was a large, violet crystal sphere, slightly bigger than a softball. To my surprise, I saw sparks of golden light emanating from it. I started to back out to give Nakoa some privacy, but he raised a hand to beckon me inside.

"Come inside, Sister." He turned to face me with a gentle smile and gestured at a round meditation pillow next to him.

I kept my eyes on the glowing sphere. "What is that?" I asked.

"A witness."

I raised my eyebrows.

"In ancient times, we performed the ho'oponopono ceremony with a live sea creature as a witness and scribe. In modern times, we use a healing crystal." He nodded at the sphere. "You may touch it."

I reached out hesitantly and brushed my fingertips over the smooth, cool surface. A jolt of electricity singed my fingers, and I yanked my hand away.

"Yes, it is alive. All things have life energy," Nakoa said. "You see… that is why your sensitivity is essential." His eyes met mine, and I looked away.

Tears welled up in my eyes.

"What is it, sister?"

My throat tightened. I didn't know how to explain to him how much his loving acceptance meant. That throughout my life, I struggled to be *seen*.

"My aunt used to scold me for being too sensitive. I learned to repress that side of me."

"I understand."

I looked up at him and could feel that he had gone through something similar.

"How do we persevere?"

He tapped his chest. "By living from *here*. To lead from your heart keeps you strong."

We fell into a silent reverie together, gazing at the glowing sphere.

He broke the silence first. "Where is your man?"

"He's finishing his dinner."

I thought enviously of Rodrigo eating his third piece of Shara's banana bread as I'd slipped away. I had been tuned out all during dinner, thinking about Rodrigo's imminent departure. I had second thoughts about staying longer. As I left, I heard him jokingly saying Shara's cooking was the main thing he'd miss about leaving the lodge.

"It's common to have fears about the unknown." Nakoa said.

"It's not just *that*." I paused. "I don't like feeling exposed and vulnerable. I never considered it a strength."

"Sister, you are a *wahine koa*—a warrior. Never forget that."

Tears spilled down my face. I didn't know how to process his kind words.

Rodrigo's quiet entrance startled me. The gentle camaraderie that Nakoa and I shared shifted when he entered the yurt. I felt a sting of resentment, but it quickly dissipated as he smiled fondly at me. Nakoa gestured to the meditation pillow on his other side, and Rodrigo sat down. I reached over and took his hand and squeezed it. He winked at me.

Nakoa cleared his throat. "Before we begin, I would like to share what my good friend Aunty Mahealani Henry expressed so eloquently. "*Ho'oponopono Pono Ke Ala* is passed down through family lineage. The one word *Ho'ponopono* is a popular version, which emphasizes forgiveness. However, what I was taught by my own elder is our familial version is about acceptance. I feel it is appropriate for me to share this with you before you are married. I will demonstrate." Nakoa cleared his throat. "Please listen and repeat back. I am a kupuna. I invite you to accept me as a kupuna. Please support me as a kupuna.. Thank you. I love you."

I nervously cleared my throat. My heart raced and my cheeks got warm as I self-consciously faced Nakoa. "You are a kupuna. I accept you as a kupuna. I support you as a kupuna. Thank you. I love you."

Nakoa smiled with approval. "Noelani. You may start. Please face Rodrigo."

My stomach tightened nervously. "I am a…"

"Changeling," Nakoa whispered.

"I am a changeling. I invite you to accept me as a changeling. Please support me as a changeling. Thank you. I love you."

Rodrigo cleared his throat. "You are a changeling. I accept you as a changeling. I support you as a changeling. Thank you. I love you."

My heart bloomed as his words washed over me tenderly. The kindness in Rodrigo's words made my eyes well up with tears. All the pent up tension I'd felt for weeks melted away. He reached over and entwined his fingers with mine. The crystal flickered briefly as though bestowing a benediction.

This is my soulmate, my partner for life. The absolute certainty of our union vibrated inside me.

Nakoa gestured at Rodrigo, who looked uncertainly at us both. "I am a healer. I invite you to accept me as a healer. Please support me as a healer. Thank you. I love you."

My throat closed up with the intensity I felt. I cleared my throat and paused. Nakoa nodded reassuringly, and his steady gaze imbued me with confidence. I calmly repeated the words back to Rodrigo. His eyes filled with tears. He quickly wiped them away with the back of his hand. The crystal flickered again. We joined both our hands together. A powerful life force pulsed through our fingertips, and a heat permeated our joined palms.

"*Aloha ke akua,*" Nakoa murmured. He leaned over and joined our hands together. "The ancestors are pleased. Can you feel their love? Can you feel the love of Mother Earth in this sacred space? We are blessed tonight."

A ticklish sensation fanned over my body. It was like I'd consumed an entire bottle of champagne. A joyous lightness flowed through me. More tears streamed down my face. It was indescribable.

Chapter Eighteen

The morning was a blur, with me driving Rodrigo to the airport in the lodge van after breakfast. Kailani and Shara were busy baking mango muffins and banana bread for the food booth at Uncle Robert's tonight. Rodrigo said his farewells to the lodge staff hurriedly over breakfast, and then we were off to the Hilo airport. Instead of being excited about his new job, he was irate and frustrated.

"I can't believe HR screwed up my paperwork," Rodrigo fumed.

"Just resubmit it when you get there. I'm sure it's not a big deal."

"After everything they put me through—the long ass background check, checking my references, submitting to a drug test, and now they can't find my application. I'm glad I have proof I sent it."

"At least they sent you the offer letter on time. *That* was worrying me."

He was intently scrolling through his messages on his phone.

"I knew they couldn't screw that up. I heard that I was their top pick for the job."

"Just think… next time you get on the plane, we'll officially be *husband and wife!*"

"Hey, I forgot to add you on the benefits package… *shit.* I totally spaced out. And the W-2 should have included you too." He shook his head in frustration. "Too many moving parts," he moaned.

"I'm sure you can add me later. You're just not used to this whole marriage thing!"

"I guess you're right. Ooooof… what a weird feeling."

I tilted my head to one side and narrowed my eyes. *Weird?*

Rodrigo shook himself and put his hand over mine. "Sorry…that came out wrong." He leaned over and kissed me lightly. I thought I'd feel teary-eyed and sad at his departure, but I was actually looking forward to spending my last few days at the lodge with just Kailani and Shara. I had never experienced this side of Rodrigo. After stressing about finding the perfect work outfits, he became vexed and impatient over the non-stop HR paperwork. When I pulled up to the airport curb, Rodrigo hopped out with his backpack. I climbed out, and we stood and embraced awkwardly.

"I'm going to miss you," he said.

"I'll see you back here in a week for the wedding."

"*I know that…* but can't I miss my woman?"

We exchanged a rushed kiss amidst the busy and congested airport traffic. I watched him hurry into the Hawaiian Airlines terminal as I pulled away from the curb.

***

The luminous, flaxen, full moon hung low in the inky night sky. I was walking to the meditation yurt to meet Braydon, who was finishing up a private yoga session. The air was still steamy, and my cotton tank top clung to my damp skin. Thankfully, I had on loose cotton yoga pants. My flipflops made a crunching sound on the rough, gravel path. It was the only palpable sound in the still night. I climbed up the short, wooden steps of the yurt, kicked off my sandals, and opened the door. The scent of jasmine incense surrounded me as I stepped inside. I saw Braydon kneeling at the wooden altar in prayer. He turned to look at me. His face was contorted in a frightening grimace.

"You don't belong here," he hissed.

Then I saw the stained glass chapel window over the altar. A beam of incandescent light illuminated the brightly colored glass. An unexpected chill rippled through me. My stomach twisted with fear. *What the hell is going on?* Suddenly, the stained glass window and Braydon dissolved in a white, shimmering light. *Holy shit... what just happened?* I put my hand over my heart to calm my pounding chest. Then a familiar but startling noise jostled me. It was Ozzie barking and clawing at the front door. I moved over to the door and pushed it open as Ozzie darted in frantically. He jumped on my legs, his sharp nails clawing at my shins.

"Ozzie!" I leaned over and picked him up to quiet him, but he anxiously squirmed around. His mood matched mine as I looked around the empty yurt. *Where is everyone? Where is Braydon? Did I get the time wrong?* The yurt door banged open with a thud, and I looked up to see Braydon standing in the doorway. Ozzie leapt out of my arms and ran to Braydon. He began to yip happily, his big brown eyes fixed on him, his tail wagging vigorously.

"There you are!" he said.

"What happened to your yoga session?" I asked.

"She was a no show, so I went down to Turtle Beach to meditate."

"*At night?* That trail is tricky enough during the day."

"I'm part goat, didn't you know that?"

"And… it's damn spooky down there. That time Lono took me there, I felt some weird *juju*."

"You probably picked up on the *aumakua* or the Mo'o… water dragons that protect the water. They're actually pretty nice."

"You commune with water dragons?"

"Doesn't everyone?" he joked. "Hey, are you okay? You've got some serious chicken skin going on!"

"You won't believe what just happened. I had this weird… I don't know… *vision*."

I described what I saw, and he listened attentively. When I finished, he pursed his lips and stared off pensively.

"I actually dreamt of this moment," Braydon said.

"*You did?*"

He gazed over my shoulder above the altar.

"I saw you standing at the altar with the stained glass window above it. Maybe you had a timeline shift—like you jumped ahead and saw a future event."

I shook my head. "That sounds like a sci-fi movie. It only lasted seconds. If I could actually time travel, I'd skip the wedding and be in California already," I joked.

"*Girl…* you can't skip your own damn wedding. Come on, now!" Braydon looked so shocked, it made me laugh aloud.

"I've already been married before, so it's not a big deal."

"Yeah, but you haven't been married to *Rodrigo* before."

A pleasant warmth rippled through me at his kind words. I put my hand on Braydon's shoulder and gave him an affectionate squeeze. "You're right. Thanks for putting things into perspective."

"Maybe we should get going to Uncle Robert's," Braydon said.

We headed out toward the main lodge where the shuttle van was parked. Braydon climbed into the van and started the engine as I hopped in simultaneously.

He winked at me and started to back the van down the driveway. As we headed out on the main road, I wondered about that vision. *What is it telling me? What does it mean?*

***

As always, Uncle Robert's was bustling with music, people and food. Braydon pulled over to drop me off in front.

"I'll meet you inside," he said.

I jumped out and made my way through the throng of laughing, mostly inebriated partygoers. The pungent smell of marijuana smoke was thick in the air. Shara and Kailani had left earlier to set up their food booth. I had helped them load cardboard boxes of bagged mango muffins, banana bread, and sachets of herbal tea. I scanned the booths for the lodge sign or any signs of Kailani and Shara. A quartet of Hawaiian slack key guitar players crooned a familiar song. A wave of nostalgia flooded me as I threaded through the crowd. I recognized a few smiling faces, who waved or nodded in my direction. I thought about the time I'd bumped into Jason here and danced with him. It seemed so long ago. *Another lifetime ago.*

I heard someone calling my name and looked up to see Kailani waving her arms over her head. To her right, to my utter shock, Cassie held up a signboard that read, *"Mrs. Rodrigo Santos."*

What is going on?

Standing behind them were Diana, Lulu, and Shara. They rushed toward me and we came together in a clumsy group hug.

"You guys!" I blurted.

"Boy, did we get you good," Diana teased.

"What are you guys doing here? Oh my God… I can't believe this."

"You said you didn't want a bridal shower, but we decided you needed one," Shara said with a grin.

"You skipped it the last time!" Kailani added.

Cassie leaned over and hugged me tightly. "You need some fun."

My eyes welled up with tears as I took in the beaming faces of my sweet friends. Lulu grabbed my hand and squeezed it. "I'm so happy you're coming back to California. Too bad my daughter decided to move the family to Vegas. I hope you'll come visit. California's hella closer to Vegas."

It was so much to take in.

Kailani took my wrist and guided me to a table they had set up nearby. Everything was festooned in shades of pink. On top of the wooden table were simple flower arrangements of fuchsia orchids, orange lilies ,and green ferns in tall water glasses. A large, glass bowl of pink punch with raspberries, sliced strawberries, and pineapple chunks sat in the center of the table. A huge pink and white balloon bouquet floated above the table. Pink, wooden, folding chairs were placed around the table with pink cushions.

"Enough pink for 'ya?" Diana joked.

"Cassie did all this!" Kailani said.

Cassie shook her head and waved at the group. "It was a team effort. The hardest part was luring you here under false pretenses."

"Come sit down," Lulu said.

I went over to the table and sat as Shara poured me some pink punch. I took a sip of the cool fruity drink.

"I'm overwhelmed… *thank you.* It's amazing to have us all here."

Cassie sat down next to me and squeezed my knee fondly. "I'm so excited you're coming back. We can hang out again!"

As I surveyed the group, I realized they were all wearing pink tank tops that said "*Mrs. Rodrigo Santos.*"

Cassie caught my gaze and pushed a pink gift bag into my hands. "I almost forgot."

I pulled out pink tissue paper to find my own pink tank top. Tears again welled in my eyes as I held the shirt against my chest. "I don't know what to say."

"Don't start blubbering now," Diana said.

"There's pink cake to eat!" Lulu said.

"Where's Braydon… isn't he part of this?" I asked.

"Behind you, sweetie, and look who I found!" Braydon said.

I turned to see Lono, grinning and wearing a matching pink tank top. He hugged me from behind and kissed the top of my head.

Shara offered Lono and Braydon glasses of pink punch.

Kailani lifted her own glass and said, "To the former Noelani Lee and the new *Mrs. Rodrigo Santos!*"

There were enthusiastic cheers as we all clinked glasses of pink punch.

Mrs. Rodrigo Santos. Wow. The shit just got real.

Chapter Nineteen

"I'm going to miss this!" I said.

Kailani grinned as she dipped her wooden spoon into her giant mound of shaved ice. It was a monolith of pink and cream iciness, with juicy red, sliced strawberries, crowned with a tall swirl of whipped cream. I had no idea where she packed all the calories she consumed daily. I looked at my own modest bowl of mango shaved ice, which was much smaller. There were bright chunks of orange mango topped with a dollop of vanilla ice cream. I'd wanted to splurge calorie-wise, but I still had to get into the vintage wedding dress I bought shopping at the Haight. It was a stunning blush-colored, lace, tea-length dress with a halter neckline. I realized with a pang of regret that my bathing suit bottoms were getting snug. I sighed as I spooned some mango into my mouth.

"Thanks for arranging a quick trip here," I said.

Kailani waved her wooden ice cream spoon at me. "*Of course. It's your last weekend as a single lady.*"

"I'm glad we could hang out together."

"The stars aligned—I got two massage gigs, and the rental house was free… so, *all good*."

"I guess Rodrigo's new job really impacted your work life." I was referring to the fact that Kailani was back to doing outcall massage in Honolulu.

"I missed my clients, honestly," she sighed. "Plus, Diana's coming back to run the lodge, so I don't have to do that anymore. She's better at it than me anyway. By the way, I have a proposition."

I raised my eyebrows.

"How'd you like to be our official social media manager?"

"I thought that spot was already taken?"

"If you mean Shara's niece, she's moved on. You'd be perfect since you've actually stayed at the lodge and know it so well. The pay sucks, though!" she chuckled.

I liked the idea of staying connected to the lodge.

"Sure."

"Really?"

"I'm going to turn into Cassie 2.0—posting every day," I joked. It was a fun thought, and I was glad Kailani had proposed the idea. "I'm also feeling untethered right now. And… after what happened to Dr. Serena, I'm feeling unsettled."

Dr. Serena couldn't come officiate at the wedding at the last minute. She had fallen and broke her hip in her driveway.

"Yeah, I was sorry to hear that, sweetie."

"I keep forgetting how old she is."

I stared off into the distance to quell the disquieting sensation in the pit of my stomach. I had counted on Dr. Serena to be there. It was an unexpected letdown. There were other unexpected issues as well. Rodrigo refused to accept Margot's generous wedding cash, and we ended up donating it all to the Maui Strong charity, which I was happy about. Nonetheless, his stubborn resistance to not accept a gift from his mother felt hurtful. Also, with his new work schedule, we decided it was more practical to do an abbreviated honeymoon with a three-day weekend in Napa.

"I'm glad that he's excited about his new job, but I wish he'd put in more time for our honeymoon."

"He'll make it up to you," Kailani said.

I didn't know how to explain the sinking loss I was feeling. Leaving the islands, starting fresh in the Bay Area wasn't an adventure I was looking forward to. I knew Kailani could leap into the unknown with zeal and finesse, but navigating new vistas wasn't for me. I always felt like the nerdy new girl on the first day of high school.

"Come on, lets enjoy today. The wedding is still a week away!" she said.

I smiled for her sake. *I don't want to leave*—why can't she understand that? My BFF had an enviable knack of embracing each moment with gusto. I wished I could be more like her, but gracefully regrouping wasn't my superpower.

***

A few days later, Kailani and I picked Rodrigo up together in the lodge van after stopping for lodge supplies at Costco. I was so happy to see him standing at the airport curb. He looked sharp in his light-blue, thin-striped polo shirt over blue chino trousers and sandals. He wore his aviator sunglasses, which gave him a mysterious but sexy vibe. I appreciated that he always dressed stylishly when we traveled. I didn't like the grungy look of most tourists in their baggy t-shirts, denim shorts, and stained running shoes.

"There's *your man!*" Kailani said. "Damn, he looks extra hot."

I raised my eyebrows.

"I can still admire a fine looking dude," Kailani added. She tooted the van horn, and he looked up with a smile. That familiar, genuine smile that made me feel gooey inside. She pulled the van over, and I slid the door open and hopped out. I jumped on him, and he lifted me up as I wrapped my legs around his waist. He kissed me thoroughly, and a thrilling ripple quivered through me.

"Hey, guys… *get a room!*" Kailani yelled.

"I'm so glad to see you guys," Rodrigo said.

I composed myself while he lifted his travel duffle bag and hoisted it into the back seat. Then he helped me up and slid in next to me, leaning over to shut the door.

"Did you have a good flight?" I asked.

He shrugged and grimaced. "I got spoiled when the clinic flew me out first class. Even the extra comfort seats are kind of a letdown."

"No more *steerage* for this guy," Kailani said.

She pulled the van away from the curb and merged into traffic. Rodrigo put his hand on my knee and squeezed affectionately.

"In fact, I upgraded our tickets to first class."

"Are you kidding? That's so expensive!" I said.

He shrugged. "I got a signing bonus, so why not? I'm cheating you out of a decent honeymoon, so I gotta make up for it."

Kailani grinned at me in the rearview mirror—it was her *I told you so* look.

"How're things at the lodge?" he asked.

"We're booked up with wedding guests!" Kailani said. "It's all good. Shara and I needed a break, and it's been great to catch up with Cassie and Diana."

"I saw the shower video. It was a giant pink explosion!" he said.

"Apparently, my bestie is sneakier than I give her credit for. I still don't know how you kept quiet about the shower."

Kailani laughed. "You've been so preoccupied with wedding stuff, you didn't even have a clue."

Rodrigo grinned. "It's good to be back. I'm ready for some serious canoodling with my woman!"

***

In the dream, Rodrigo and I stood at an altar, our hands clasped together. Our wrists are intricately tied together in an elaborate, woven design with thick twine. Dr. Serena was smiling at me. She put her hand on our joined wrists. *"You are bound forever. You are twin souls who have come together again in this life, as you have many times before."*

Then Dr. Serena's eyes turned dark. A loud, cacophonous roar shook the ground. Rodrigo stared at me in shock. "What's happening?" he yelled.

I jerked awake and sat up, my heart pounding. My cotton t-shirt nightgown was soaked in sweat. I forked my fingers through my damp hair.

The mischievous lodge doggo, Ozzie, was spinning around in a circle, barking. Rodrigo scooped up the furry troublemaker.

"Sorry to wake you."

I flopped back against the damp pillows with a sigh. "It's okay."

Ozzie barked defiantly and wriggled loose from Rodrigo. He landed with a thud on the floor and barked sharply at me.

"I am *not* going to miss you," I muttered. Ozzie cocked his head to one side and stared at me with confusion.

"Those big brown puppy eyes don't work on me," I said.

Rodrigo laughed and opened the front door. Ozzie scampered out, then Rodrigo came over to the bed and kissed the top of my head. "Last night was so fun." he said with a devilish grin.

"You shouldn't have snuck in. It's bad luck to see the bride before the wedding day."

"*Who says?*" He climbed in bed and snuggled up against me, spoon-style. I closed my eyes and enjoyed the feeling of his toned, supple body pressed against mine. The night before, he was supposed to stay at the lodge but had snuck into our cabin after I fell asleep. I was pleasantly awakened to find him curled up against me, his hands caressing my arms in light, soft strokes. When I rolled over to face him, he devoured me with a hungry kiss. My body had a mind of its own when I was with him. My legs automatically parted, and he rolled on top of me. He cinched the hem of my cotton nightshirt in his hand and yanked it up, over my hips.

"Ohhhhh… no panties," he whispered.

"No boxers," I replied.

"No… *nothing,*" he corrected.

He pressed his hips against mine and slid himself inside me.

"Someone was expecting me," he teased.

"No foreplay tonight?"

"Obviously, you don't need it."

My hands clutched his back as he moved deeper inside me. I felt like I was still dreaming—the dark, steamy night and the gentle sound of the coqui frogs created a surreal atmosphere. Rodrigo's pace quickened, and my legs clamped around him as he gasped and then softly moaned.

"*Sorry,*" he murmured. "I was hoping to hold out longer."

He rolled off with a sigh, and I propped myself up on my elbow. "It's been two weeks. But who's counting?"

He chuckled. "I think that's the longest we've gone."

"*Really?*"

"Really."

Now, as Rodrigo and I laid together in the early morning, a refreshing, cool breeze swept through the room. I listened to him gently snoring. In a few hours, we would officially become Mr. and Mrs. Rodrigo Santos. My old identity as Noelani Lee, divorced and single, would be transformed into Mrs. Noelani Santos, happily married wife. I softly touched Rodrigo's face as he slept.

***

My big day. I looked at my reflection in the tall, gilt swivel mirror that Lono and Braydon had installed inside the yoga yurt. They'd set up the yurt as the bridal dressing room, with the leftover folding pink chairs from the bridal shower scattered around the mirror.

"You look stunning!" Margot said. She was sitting in one of the pink chairs, sipping iced tea. It was a strange feeling seeing myself dolled up with makeup and a lacy wedding gown that was straight out of a Disney princess film. I wasn't used to wearing makeup, and the glam fake eyelashes that Cassie insisted on at the last minute felt over-the-top. Shara had braided my hair into a romantic updo and crowned the top of my head with a green ti leaf *haku*. Margot had surprised me by gifting me a three-strand pearl choker necklace with simple pearl stud earrings. She was dressed in a lacy, lavender gown with a matching fascinator hat and netting that draped over her forehead. She had cut her graying hair to chin-length, which suited her narrow face.

"I look like a drag queen," I said.

Margot got up and walked over to me. She put her hands gently on my shoulders and smiled. "You're not used to so much attention. *I totally get it.*"

"I don't think Rodrigo is going to recognize me."

"Of course he will." Margot patted my back. "This is *your day*. I want you to enjoy every moment. Kailani and Shara and the others worked hard to make it special… *for you.*"

"This is so different than my first wedding."

"Kailani said you two eloped?"

I nodded. "To Lake Tahoe."

The memory of that made me realize how different this wedding was than that impulsive elopement. At the time, it had seemed exciting and romantic, but in retrospect, it was just another sad example of me wanting to be chosen and needing to feel special. Now I was with a man who not only cared about my well-being but was stalwart in his loyalty to me. *I have definitely evolved.*

"I also eloped to Lake Tahoe… with one of my husbands. I can't think which one?" Margot sighed.

I looked over at her. *Can't remember which husband?* What was that about? Before I could comment, Braydon, our official wedding photographer, walked into the yurt with his Nikon camera. "Smile, babe!"

I heard the camera click and was startled by a brief flash. He was dressed in a white polo shirt over tan chino pants. A lei of round, dark-brown kukui nuts and the customary flip-flops completed his look.

"You look ah-mazing," Braydon said.

"Do you really need the flash?" Margot asked.

Braydon adjusted something on the camera and took another shot.

"Hmmmm… maybe we should go outside. It's time for the *first look* photos anyway!"

First look photographs, groom's cake, and elongated stem flower bouquets. All these were new concepts to me. I liked the simpler flower bouquet that Shara had designed with just four white Calla lilies with a spray of white Freesias wrapped with a simple, white, satin ribbon.

Margot picked up my bouquet off the wooden altar and presented it to me.

"I can't wait to see how Rodrigo reacts," she said.

She went over to the front door and opened it as Braydon hurried out first to get in position. My chest was thudding so hard, I thought my heart would explode. Margot smiled with encouragement as I walked through the door. I didn't expect to see Rodrigo standing there at the bottom of the stairs, beaming at me. He was dressed impeccably in a light gray suit, a crisp, white shirt with a single white orchid and green fern leaf attached to his lapel.

"*Wow*," Rodrigo said.

"Wow yourself!" I replied.

"The suit's Emporio Armani," Braydon interjected. "He borrowed it from Lono."

"*Lono owns a suit?*" I exclaimed.

"The white Converse shoes are mine," Rodrigo joked. "It looks dumb, huh?"

"I think it's fun, and you look incredibly handsome."

My face flushed as Rodrigo stared silently at me.

"My makeup… it's too much, right?" I blurted.

He shook his head with a smile. "I just can't believe I'm marrying the most beautiful woman in the world."

Rodrigo held out his hand to help me down the stairs while Braydon circled us, happily snapping away.

"Let's get the three of you together," Braydon suggested.

Margot met us at the bottom of the stairs, and we posed in front of the yurt.

"So, this is what celebrities go through," Rodrigo sighed. "I'm glad I'm not famous."

"*You love it,*" Braydon teased. "Come on… the ceremony's starting. Rodrigo, you need to get in front of the wedding arch. Let's go."

"*Yessir!*" Rodrigo said and rolled his eyes. He leaned over and kissed me on the cheek. "*I'm the luckiest man alive,*" he whispered.

Margot and I watched them leave. She took my hand. "Are you ready for your big moment?"

I was in a daze. An odd tingling swept over me. *I'm going to marry my soulmate, and our life is going to be amazing.*

"This is so…*surreal.*"

"You've got this."

The entire morning had a dreamy quality—being pampered by my loving friends, wearing a beautiful, flowing dress, and witnessing Rodrigo's genuine loving gaze. I didn't want this day to end. Margot squeezed my hand fondly… then we were off to the lodge, where the ceremony was being held.

***

They had cleared the dining patio in front of the lodge kitchen and set up a metal wedding arch topped with bright, tropical bouquets of red ginger, orange birds of paradise, and green ferns.

Lono stood under the arch to the left, wearing an identical outfit as Braydon's with a long sleeved, white shirt and tan chino trousers. Underneath the arch was Nakoa, looking dapper in all-black attire with a green ti leaf crown and a black kukui nut lei. To his right stood my future husband, smiling.

Is this really happening? I thought as I took in the scene.

One of Nakoa's friends was singing a classic Hawaiian ballad: *Kawaipunahele*. I didn't understand the words, but the haunting music brought tears to my eyes. About twenty bamboo folding chairs faced the wedding arch, and they were all occupied with our friends. I saw Cassie, Shara, and Kailani sitting in the front row. Cassie was busy mopping her eyes with tissue, with her husband Steve beside her. He gave me a playful wink and the thumbs up as we got closer. Margot slowly guided me down the grass toward the wedding arch. She kissed my forehead when we arrived in front of Nakoa. He nodded at me solemnly, then reached into his back pocket and held out his cell phone. I looked at him and then Rodrigo in confusion. Lono gestured for me to look at the phone. It was Dr. Serena, sitting in a wheelchair dressed in one of her signature silk kimono over black yoga pants.

"Aloha, my dear friend," she said. "I'm so sorry I can't be there, so I thought I'd pop in virtually. I want to share my favorite Pablo Neruda quote. *'Then love knew it was called love. And when I lifted my eyes to your name, suddenly your heart showed me my way.'* Noelani and Rodrigo… I love you both and I wish you so much happiness. Aloha." Dr. Serena clasped her hands together and bowed her head. Now my tears flowed freely.

Nakoa put his phone away, and Rodrigo reached over and rubbed my back affectionately.

Nakoa leaned toward us and said, "Please take each other's hands and repeat after me. *I promise that I will dedicate my life from this day forward to filling our days with joy and laughter. I will celebrate your spirit and remind you of your beauty and strength. I take you today as my partner, and I will love you for the rest of our days.*"

Nakoa nodded at Rodrigo. He looked into my eyes and repeated the first sentence and froze. Nakoa smiled patiently. "I will celebrate your spirit," he prompted.

"I will celebrate your spirit and remind you of your beauty and strength. I take you today as my partner, and I will love you for the rest of our days."

They both turned toward me expectantly. My mind went blank. "What *he* said!" I joked.

A ripple of laughter fanned through the audience.

"*I promise that I will dedicate my life from this day forward to filling our days with joy and laughter,*" Nakoa prompted.

This is really happening. I'm going to marry an amazing man who cherishes me and will always be my side. Together, we will build a joyful future together. I looked into Rodrigo's eyes, shining with happy tears. In this precious moment, only the two of us existed as the rest of the world faded away. I confidently repeated the rest of the vows.

"Noelani and Rodrigo. Do you take one another as partners form this day forward, as husband and wife?"

"We do."

Nakoa turned toward Lono. "Do you promise to stand by this couple, to remind them of their commitment to each other?"

Lono nodded. "I do."

Lono reached into his front pocket and produced two gold wedding rings, which he presented to both Rodrigo and me.

Nakoa cleared his throat. "Noelani and Rodrigo… you have chosen these rings to represent the unbreakable circle of life and love. Please repeat after me. I give you this ring as a reminder that I will love, honor, and cherish you in all times, in all places, and in all ways, forever."

I slipped Rodrigo's ring onto his finger, and he did the same for me.

Nakoa clasped his hands together. "It is with joy that I now send you out into the world to spread the beautiful light that you share with those around you. By the power vested in me, I now pronounce you *married*!"

Nakoa's blessing reverberated joyfully in my soul. I was filled with an indescribable lightness as my worldly concerns vanished. In this moment, everything was perfect and as it should be.

Loud, joyous applause erupted from the crowd as we kissed. It was the end of one life and the beginning of a new one. There would be more stories to tell.

COMING SOON
The Dragon Diary
Book 3 of the Pono Trilogy
@nicolasluv